F*** My Brain! is a unique and enjoyable book to read. Although the theme of being an outsider has been widely explored, the author masterfully finds fresh perspectives that make the book relevant and interesting. The book is a promising debut. Amir Shaheen is certainly a writer worth keeping an eye on. STOFFMAGASIN.NO

I was pleasantly surprised by this book. Shaheen strikes a balance between humor and seriousness, alternating between telling absurd stories and grounding them in reality. However, what they all have in common is an underlying message. The writing is fantastic, and there is general humor in most of the stories, which will appeal to a wide audience. BOKBLOGGEREN.COM

Among the absurd and peculiar stories, several important themes are addressed, such as racism, derogatory views of women, and religion. However, these topics are often presented so humorously that I can't help but chuckle to myself. As promised on the back cover, it's certainly never boring! @Bok.Ellie.

You know when your brain thinks of something out of the blue, and then it keeps associating further without you being able to control it, and suddenly it has run away with the original thought and turned it into something completely random and crazy? That's what the stories in this book remind me of – it's not afraid to venture into those weird places. I absolutely loved this

book, highly recommended! 5/5 @Norwegian_Booknerd

F*** MY BRAIN!

Amir Shaheen

F***

MY BRAIN!

To the world, you are strange!

Chapter 1 — Brain-Mush

Chapter 2 — One Brain Cell

Chapter 3 — Brain-Damage

Chapter 1

Brain-Mush

Mustafá's Timemachine

I was lying in bed with the most stunning girl in the world. She fit perfectly into my arms like a jigsaw puzzle piece. And she even told me she loved me, can you believe it? If only I could tell the boys, especially my best friend Abdi. "Bro, I just slept with the far-right politician, Liv motherfuckin' Monsen. We did it!"

They would be so impressed, they might even crown me king of the universe, king of kings. I mean, it wouldn't be as impressive if it happened in 2020, but in 1990, she was the real bomb, with that booty of hers.

Here I was lying next to 20-year-old Liv Monsen, the same year she was about to join the far-right party. It was all part of a calculated plan. My buddy Abdi and I built a time machine watch, with two batteries to power it. One to go back in time and one to get back home. My Mission? Go back in time and make Liv fall in love with a foreigner, a black guy. If I could just show her that foreigners are just regular folks with dreams and ambitions, maybe it would change the party's strong and racist attitudes in 2020. And boy, was I making progress! In just a few short weeks, Liv and I were practically a couple, and on her birthday, May 27th, I was set to meet her parents. It was a crazy time to be in, but oh so exciting. Nelson Mandela was finally released after 27 years as a political prisoner, and Nasa Launched the Hubble Space Telescope on board the Discovery space shuttle. I even got to watch MC Hammer dance on her cute little square tv. Liv called his pants cute pajama pants - she had no idea how big Hip-Hop culture would become, the rock´n´roll of the future.

"Hey, Liv, are you awake?" I asked.
"I love lying in your arms, Mustafa," she said dreamily.

I could hear the love in her voice, and I felt the same way. But at the same time, I had a knot in my stomach. Maybe it was because I knew who she was going to become, and how much I wished I could change it. The battery on my time machine watch was running low. If I was going to make it back to 2020, I had to act fast. I never would have believed I could have feelings for the infamous Liv Monsen, but there I was. I couldn't just disappear without an explanation, but with each passing moment, the elephant in the room was getting bigger and bigger. I had to tell her the truth, or maybe I didn't. The job was done, she liked foreigners now. But if I was going to come clean, it had to be today.

I was in the kitchen, watching eggs fry in the pan, trying to come up with a plan. It was anyone's guess how it would all end. I caught a glimpse of Liv, the most beautiful woman in the world, getting ready for the day. I knew I had to tell her.

"Liv?" I said hesitantly.
"Yes, my dear?" she replied.
"Can you take a seat? We need to talk."

Liv could tell from my voice that something was off. How do you tell someone you're from the future without sounding like Doc Brown from "Back to the Future"? She looked at me with concern, waiting for me to spill the beans. "Liv, there's something I need to tell you. I've been pondering this for a while, knowing that this day would come, but I never found the right moment or place to say it."

She took my hands and gave me a reassuring smile. "Just tell me, Mustafa. I can handle it." She was and is a tough cookie, and I could see why she had made it so face in her career.
I took a deep breath and blurted it out.

"Liv, I'm from the future. I know it sounds crazy, but it's true!" Liv burst out laughing. "Wow, Mustafa, you really had me going there for a second! You're such a joker. Now, what's the real news?"

"Liv, my name is Mustafa Hussein, and I was born on January 4th, 1987. Right now, I'm a three-year-old boy living in Somalia. My family moves to Oslo in 1996, and my parents do their best to give me a safe upbringing and a secure future. I study to become an engineer and get a master's degree in physics. Together with my best friend Abdi, we invented a time machine watch. I go back in time to meet you, Liv. But my time here is running out, and I can't just leave without an explanation!"

I could see that Liv thought I was joking. She stood up and took the frying pan off the stove - I had forgotten that it was still cooking our breakfast.

"Mustafa, what you're saying is pretty wild," Liv said skeptically.
"Yeah, you can say that again. But..." I began.
"Are you struggling with schizophrenia or delusions?" Liv interrupted.

The tension in the room was palpable as Liv opened and closed the refrigerator, before slamming the door shut and saying, "You think I'm stupid? Is this some sick joke you're playing to avoid meeting my parents? I...just...what the hell? Why are you saying this?"

I decided to give her some time to gather her thoughts. "Let's say you're from the future, and let's say I believe you. Why did you come back to be with me? You could have done so much more, invented things before they were actually invented, become filthy rich! You could have seen dinosaurs, seen when the pyramids were built! I don't know...maybe you've watched Back to the Future one too many times. What's so special about me?" I thought about the time travel paradox. Major changes in 1990 could lead to the time machine watch not being invented in 2020. I couldn't tell Liv too much, but maybe I could tell her what was happening in the country? Help her understand what it's like for foreigners to live in Norway?

I asked her, "When you look at me, Liv, what do you see?"

She said, "I see a handsome young man named Mustafa who I'm in love with. I see a guy who will become a great man someday. I see a guy I could spend the rest of my life with." I was in shock. Had I messed up the timeline and ended up stuck in 1990? I got nervous and kissed her. But then I had to break it to her gently. "Liv, in the future, you wouldn't be saying these things. You, your party, and especially the internet trolls would be saying..."

Liv cut me off, "What? Do we have trolls in the future?" I explained, "No, they're just idiots on the internet who like to spew hate. But the point is, Liv, in the future, you wouldn't see Mustafa. You would see a FOREIGNER. A BLACK MAN." Liv was taken aback. "Stop it..."

"I'm not mad at you, Liv. Well, actually, I am mad at you in the future. I'm sorry if I'm rambling, but I have to be careful about what I say. In the future, you would say that foreigners are Norwegian on paper, but not in their hearts. Liv, I want you to know one thing. Do you know what language me and all my foreign friends think in?"

Liv shook her head. "I don't know, Norwegian?"

"Yes, we think in Norwegian. My inner voice has always been Norwegian, I can't remember ever thinking in Somali. My home is Norway, I grew up in Stovner, and this is where I have lived my whole life. All my friends are called Paki´s, Arab´s, Neger´s or Asian´s...we all think in Norwegian. If there was a war, we would all queue up to die for Norway because this is the country we know and come from, even though we're told to get out. Where should I go, back to Stovner? If I went back to Somalia, I wouldn't survive a day. I can't read, write or speak Somali, my brain is not Somali."

Liv seemed to have forgotten that I was talking about the future, but now she was listening, and her arms, which had been tightly crossed, fell to the side of her body. As soon as the conversation took on a political tone, it was easy to get her to listen. "It's not my fault that my parents chose to move to Norway. Or, I'm wrong, they had no choice. If they hadn't left, we would have been killed. And we can't choose where we're born or what skin color we get. That's just how the genes of my parents and ancestors are, and I can't change that. There are so many foreigners with different backgrounds and skin colors who feel this way. Norwegian in the heart, foreign on the outside...In 30 years from now, you'll accuse foreigners of not having Norwegian values because there are many who don't learn the language. I want you to understand that it's not easy for many foreigners to learn Norwegian. Many come here when they're old, many come with children and feel their lives are over, and many fall into depression because they had to flee from their country. Yes, there are idiots who may come here to exploit the system, but there are also plenty of Norwegian people who do that too. In the future, you will say that Norwegians can't get jobs because of foreigners, that we come to take their jobs. I can't remember taking anyone's job. All foreigners who want a job must be equally qualified, if not more, to get the same job. You have to understand that no foreigners run into the office and just take your job. It would just be crazy, 'Hey, what are you doing here?' 'No, I was told that foreigners can just take your job, so I came here for your job. Boom, your job is now mine.'"

Liv laughed at my joke. "You're pretty funny, Mustafa," she said, still giggling.

"What are you doing, Liv?" I asked.

"I'm taking notes of what you're saying. You have some good arguments that people need to hear and know about," she replied. I took her notebook, ripped out the page, and ate it.

"Why did you do that?!" she exclaimed.

"As I said, Liv, time paradox. I can't change the past too much. I can't change you too much. I hope it will make you a better leader in the future, I know," I explained.

"I thought we were done with the time travel stuff now," she said.

"Don't you listen? I've been talking about the future the whole time? I'm from the future! And I have to go back! You and I, we can never live happily ever after. Do you understand that?" I yelled.

"Now you're scaring me, Mustafa!" she said, reaching for her phone. "What are you doing?" I demanded.

"I'm calling an ambulance, you're not well," she said, dialing the number. I grabbed her phone and threw it against the wall. "You're not listening! I can't leave without you knowing why. Liv, I love you!"

"Okay, you need to calm down because this is getting out of hand," she said, looking worried. "I have to go to work now, let's talk about this tonight."

"Fine, we'll talk tonight," I said.

I had pushed her too far. She didn't believe me. She kissed me, and only I knew that it would be our last kiss. She smiled at me before closing the door behind her. I was left alone, sad that the scenario I least hoped for had just happened. Her notebook lay on the kitchen counter next to the burnt eggs.

Dear Liv,

By the time you're reading this, I've already hopped back to 2020. I know I left without really sorting things out between us, and for that, I'm sorry. Those few weeks we spent together were some of the best of my life. Although we can't be together, I hope you'll remember us as the real deal and carry that with you as you move forward in your career. And if you still don't believe me, then take this: Norway qualifies for the 1998 Football World Cup and beats Brazil 2-1. Boom! If you ever want to find me in the future, I'll be back at my apartment on December 25th, 2020, at 12:30 pm - an hour after I left for the past.

With love,
Mustafa

I strapped on my timepiece, dialed in the year, and hit the little red button. Puff! My body and atoms were sucked through the time hole, and Puff! I was back in Abdi's room.

Abdi was waiting with a bucket, and we both knew what was coming next. Burnt eggs and yesterday's coffee now decorated the bucket's interior. Two painkillers were already waiting for the headache that would hit me in 3, 2, 1...

My head was pounding like a jackhammer, and I needed something to numb the pain. "Ahh... my head!" I groaned. Abdi handed me some pills, but they were useless against the feeling of rejection that was bubbling up inside me. I wished he had come with me. It was surreal. Liv Monsen had actually slept with a black guy! "So... did you get laid with Liv? Liv Monsen?" Abdi asked with a smirk on his face. I nodded, my sly grin confirming it. I couldn't help feeling a little bit proud of myself. Liv Monsen, the unattainable, had fallen for me. But then Abdi dropped the bombshell: "Okay, dude. Don't freak out, but it didn't work."

He pointed to the laptop, and I scrolled down, reading article after article filled with strong and racist comments. Had it all been for nothing? Were the best weeks of my life just a lie? A new form of nausea began to rise in my throat. Did I mean nothing to her?

"Even though it didn't work this time, we can try to make more batteries. We just need to think a little differently, go even further back in time," Abdi suggested optimistically. But I couldn't hear him. Even though it had been 30 years, it had only been a few hours since we were panting and gasping in each other's faces. My phone buzzed, and a message from an unknown number popped up on the screen. Abdi picked it up and read it out loud, "Mustafa, have you told anyone about the time machine watch?" I was too lost in my own thoughts to respond. As we looked out the window, we saw a big black car parked in front of the entrance. My heart sank as I caught a glimpse of Liv's bright hair through the window. "Liv..."

I muttered as I ran towards the car. But even though I had been hoping to see her again, seeing her 30 years older was a shock. The smoke had taken its toll, and her face was now covered in large pores and bad skin. As tradition dictates, she had cut her hair short, like every other 50-year-old woman, and it was filled with enough hair wax, foam, and spray to clog an entire swimming pool. She nervously ruffled the back of her head.

"Hey, Mustafa," Liv said, as she extended her hand out of the car window. I took her hand, and a chill ran down my spine. "I'm so sorry I had to leave so suddenly. I wish things could've been different." Liv's eyes turned cold. "Yeah, it wasn't exactly a blast coming home to an empty apartment."

"I apologize," I said, tears welling up in my eyes. My gaze drifted to her other hand, and my heart dropped. "Liv... is that a gun?"

With a tight grip on the revolver, she spat out bitterly, "I gave you everything, Mustafa. My whole being. And you just left? Who do you think you are? No one turns their back on me. NO ONE!"

Filled with adrenaline, she aimed the gun at my chest. "Honestly, I never thought of immigrants as a problem. But thanks to your big blow-up, I had enough material to split an entire nation."

"Liv, what are you saying? You can't..."

"Thank you, Mustafa," she interrupted, grinning greedily. "Thank you for kick-starting my career, thank you for making me a multimillionaire after I bet on the football game between Norway and Brazil, and thank you for giving me your time-machine watch." Three men dressed in black suits approached the car.

I grabbed Liv's wrinkled face and pulled it out of the car window before I punched her in the face and ran back to my apartment with the Matrix agents hot on my tail.

"Yo, that bitch is crazy! She wants our time-machine watch. We gotta destroy it!"

"What the hell? Destroy it? Why? We still have two batteries left. Let's go back in time and kill baby Liv Monsen!" The door was kicked in, and Liv calmly walked into the room with large, angry white men on each side of her. Abdi and I stood in the living room, ready to go back in time. "Mustafa!" she shouted angrily. Blood was running down her face. Her nose was probably broken and already swelling up. The men aimed their guns at us. With a small click on the time machine watch, the drama that had just unfolded would hopefully never happen. "Why, Liv?" I didn't want to leave without an explanation. Did none of what we had together mean anything to her?

"I was furious when I found the note you left for me – it couldn't be true, could it? But when I couldn't find anyone registered by the name of Mustafa Hussein in 1990, and watched Back To The Future again, I understood everything. You want to take over the whole country! I couldn't be the cause of Norway's downfall!"

"No, not quite...or what the hell?"

"Mustafa, you must hand over the time machine clock to me and the Norwegian government right away. It's not something that should be owned by a private individual. We can't have you two running around changing everything you don't like. It's something we in the government should have control over. So we can get rid of all you blacks," she said, laughing wickedly.

I looked shocked at Liv. Where was the girl I met? The good girl with the warm laughter, sweet smile, and perfect hand around... Blood had hardened and was stuck between her teeth. "Mustafa. Give me the time machine watch." She pulled out her revolver again and fired a warning shot into the ground. "I'm not kidding, before you can press that little button, we've already shot you, five times in the head and once in the heart."

The power of almost owning a time machine watch and carrying a loaded revolver had gone to her head. But we couldn't give up the time machine clock, or they would do some Handmaid's Tale shit and turn Norway into a Nazi state. "Give me the damn time machine clock!"

Abdi and I looked at each other. Both knew what had to be done. With a sly grin, we pressed the button. "See you soon Liv, see you on May 27," I said and winked arrogantly, "in 1969."
It took a while for her to understand where we were going and what we were going to do. She pulled out her revolver and shot at me as much as she could. Now it wasn't the blood that made her face red, but anger and hatred for what we were about to do. As the atoms were turned into a liquid mass and prepared for a journey through time and space, the bullets flew through us. "FUCKING FOREIGNERS," she yelled. "FUCKING NEGER`S!!"

Puff, and we were gone.

Incident at the Zoo

Reporter: "Here I am in one of the world's largest animal parks, where you can find animals from all over the world. I'm here because of the terrible incident that happened yesterday with the famous blogger Donna Pella. Donna Pella lost two fingers when she tried to take a selfie with the tiger Blondie. I have just been informed that Donna Pella is ready to talk to us live from her hospital bed.

Live from the hospital.

Donna Pella: "My life is over! Oh my god, how am I going to be able to blog now? Look at my hand! Just so you know, you stupid tiger, I'm going to sue you for everything you own! And not only that, I also want you to be put to sleep, it's not enough punishment that you live in captivity and in a cage."

Back to the zoo.

Reporter: "As you can see, Donna Pella is not taking this lightly. But there are always two sides to the same story, and that's why we want to hear what the animals in the zoo have to say about this. Let's start with the monkeys who were witnesses to the entire event. I warn all viewers in advance that this might get graphic. According to the zoo, the monkeys never learned proper manners or etiquette before they were kidnapped from their home in the jungle. So yes, I'm standing here by the monkey cage and..." Monkey Willy snatches the microphone from the reporter's hand.

Willy: "Mic-check, one two, one two... Is this thing on? Yeah? Ask me what you want to know then!"

Reporter: "What do you have to say about the incident that occurred here yesterday, with Donna Pella and the Tiger Blondie?"

Willy: "I mean, what was she thinking? Even us monkeys know not to take selfies with a tiger. It's not a dog that wants cuddles, it's a bloodthirsty kitty cat that kills for fun! Aren't you humans supposed to be smarter than all of us other animals? That Donna doesn't seem particularly smart!"

Reporter: "But did Blondie the tiger need to eat her fingers?"

Willy: "Did she need to stick her prepubescent dick fingers in his mouth?"

In the same moment, a steaming, freshly laid vegan cable poop is thrown at the reporter and the rest of the crew.

Willy: "Ew... Is that yesterday's banana peel I see on your shoulder? Sorry about that. Scarface isn't part of our troop, plays too much with his butt. He came here last month from a laboratory. The humans had apparently given him shitloads of LSD, and now he can only say: hate, bad, and human. So tragic... How about doing a report on that instead? Humans experimenting and torturing animals?"

The reporter is at a loss for words.

Willy: "No offense, buddy, but isn't that what journalism is all about? Actual news and not something that's completely obvious? This ain't no Disney movie, this is real life."

Reporter: "I know this is reality, but..."

Willy: "Oh, I love it when I'm right! Check yourself before you wreck yourself, 'cause monkey poop is bad for your health."

Willy smirks arrogantly at the reporter and runs off with the microphone to the cool gang of monkeys waiting for him a few meters away. They chant in unison: "Boys, boys, boys,

boys!" Willy holds the microphone like a trophy as they high-five and slap each other on the butt.

Reporter: "Uh, also, how are we going to get the microphone out of the cage now?" The reporter turns to the camera and retrieves a spare microphone. "Sorry for the interruption. It seems Willy has finished his interview, so we'll just move on. I'm now getting word that the tiger Blondie has come out of her cage and is ready to tell her side of what happened yesterday."

Blondie stretches and lies down in her favorite spot, the only patch of green grass in the entire enclosure. The sound guy extends a long microphone and lowers it down.

Reporter: "Blondie, what do you have to say in your defense about biting off the fingers of the famous blogger Donna Pella?"

Blondie: "Is she Italian?"

Reporter: "No."

Blondie: "I'm not an object, I'm a living being with feelings and complexities. Does she even know my good side? Did she bother to ask? I have an image too: big, tough, and dangerous. I looked like a wimp in her pictures."

Reporter: "So you felt insulted?"

Blondie: "Yes, of course I did. This is my private space, no one comes in here without my permission. I have a reputation to uphold! Look over there, at the big sign with the red letters. IT IS DANGEROUS TO CLIMB OVER. I did exactly what was expected of me, and I'm not disappointed in myself."

Suddenly, Blondie, the reporter, and the rest of the crew hear screaming. People are frantically running towards the cameraman, trying to get to the exit. With the help of the microphone, the monkeys had picked the lock and let all the animals out of the zoo.

Zookeeper: "Sound the alarm, the animals are loose! The police need to come here right away, and they need to be armed!"

Willy: "Cameraman! CAMERAMAN! Film me! Hello world. It's official, Willy is free! We're not planning on running away, we're not stupid. None of us have any idea how to survive outside the zoo. So from now on, the animals are in control of the zoo, and it's open when it suits us. All humans must leave, NOW."

The reporter picks up the camera and speaks directly to all the viewers: "This is a historic moment, the animals have kicked us out of the zoo. Dangerous animals could be anywhere, but if we just treat them with dignity and respect, I'm pretty sure they won't harm us."

The reporter and the crew film as the apes release Blondie

the tiger. All the animals bow down to the dangerous, but respected tiger. It's like something out of The Lion King.

Willy: "You, reporter woman! If you want to come back and film real news, just slide into my DMs! We have a lot to talk about! Animal abuse, plastic in the ocean, and deforestation! So much you humans have messed up. The list is long, homie!"

Unexpected Visit

Monday

Finally, it's my weekend off and boy, am I going to celebrate it. When I come home from work, I'm going to jump right into my sweatpants, dive into my hoodie with curry stains, and watch Avengers: Endgame at the cinema, all by myself. For once, I'm going to have a peaceful weekend, and no matter who calls and how tempting it is, I'm not going out. This weekend is all about me!

Wait. It can actually get even better.

I'm going to binge-watch the series I've always wanted to watch. I'll make myself proper food, no pre-mixed curry, no, that's fake news. Here, the chicken will be marinated in real garam masala, and the naan bread will be made from scratch.

After work on Monday:
Friend: "Yo, Amir. I have a meeting in Oslo on Friday, can I crash at your place this weekend? Then we can go out and get drunk like in the good old days!"
Amir: "Yeah, sure."

Tuesday
Shitshitshitshitshit. Fuck. Maybe I can call and say I'm having some girls over? No, I can't. Then he'll come for sure. Maybe I can jump in front of a car? One that's driving slowly, but fast enough to break my pinky toe?

No, bad idea.

Then he'll come to check if I'm okay. Then my whole family will come to check if I'm okay. Then they'll want me to move back home and live there until I'm better, and then I'm stuck, stuck like a nut in a nutcracker.

Wednesday
Maybe I should call the airport and say there's a bomb on his flight? No, I can't!? I took it too far.

It's so easy to trace phone calls today... They'll kick down the door and arrest me before I have time to flush down yesterday's chicken curry. And think how embarrassing it will be when they go through my log and see the latest Google searches: *How to get rid of a body. Clever places to hide small bombs. Do imams watch porn?*

Then I'll be labeled as a terrorist. When I say I'm not a terrorist, they'll just think I'm a gay terrorist with suppressed feelings who actually wants to become an imam. And because I'm not white, it will be impossible to say anything against it. WorldNews: "Police killed a non-Norwegian homosexual, soon-to-be imam, now dead, terrorist in self-defense." What a media uproar it's going to be. Poor mom. No, it's too stressful.

Thursday

Can't the world be hit by a pandemic, so the whole country goes into lockdown? Oh... yeah... Then I can be completely alone, without worrying about any uninvited guests, and watch and eat exactly what I want! Then I can sit in my favorite spot at IMAX and watch Avengers!

But... wouldn't the cinema also be closed then? Nah, that doesn't sound very likely. Oh my God, I've watched too many disaster movies.

Friday

Amir: "Yo, good to see you! Glad you came to visit."
Buddy: "Come on, let's go out for some beers!"

Amir and his buddy have a few drinks, and after a few, it turns into a few more. Eventually, the rest of the gang shows up and they hit the town. With great music, colorful strobe lights, a shot in one hand and a beer in the other, all the worries of the week are forgotten.

On the way home, they grab a kebab.
Both: "Damn, that was fun!"

Saturday
Amir: "Good morning, buddy!"
Buddy: "Good morning! Beer?"
Amir: "Let's do it!" Many hours later...
Amir: "Buddy...why haven't we done this before? I've missed you, man!"

Sunday morning
Amir: "That was a sick weekend, so glad you came!"
Oh well, it wasn't so bad after all. I will have time off soon enough! It's not like Avengers: Endgame is going anywhere and the series I plan to binge-watch will still be there.

Rapper

The young, pubescent Rapper had been bullied his whole life. So ugly was he that he had never experienced his first kiss, and he had never had a real friend. What nobody knew was that he had an ear for music. Writing and producing songs was his way of escaping reality because here, nobody could say mean things about what he created. Thus, the magical tones were created, and that's why music was his one true love.

After school was over and everyone was off to learn how to become adults, the Rapper was left in his basement with a sea of songs nobody had heard. He played these over and over again on full blast on his sound system and dreamed himself into an alternate universe where he had signed a record deal with Sony and could choose from the most beautiful women in the world.

But it wasn't just the Rapper who daydreamed to his music.

The Outsider, a new kid in the neighboring house, heard the enchanting, almost poetic melodies. No matter how much he tried to Shazam the songs, he got nowhere. The Outsider had to know where he could find these songs! With three quick knocks on the door, the Outsider mustered the courage to ask the neighbor. The Rapper cautiously opened the door and peeked through a small crack. A good friend is hard to come by. The Rapper and the Outsider might have had to wait longer than most people, but when they finally met, they were inseparable.

"You have to release your music, people need to hear this!" The Rapper was happy to see the Outsider so engaged. But the Rapper didn't want to show his face in front of people again, he was afraid of being bullied. He didn't want to be laughed at, he had had enough of that. The Outsider could relate to what the Rapper was talking about, and came up with a plan. "Why not upload your music anonymously? Let me become your manager, and I'll take care of everything for you. You can just relax and do what you're best at, making otherworldly, utterly brilliant music!" The Rapper accepted this with one criterion: it wouldn't be at the expense of their friendship. So the Outsider got a song he could upload on the big World Wide Web.

Like wildfire, the song spread to all continents. Who was this secret artist? Where did he come from? All the questions made the song even hotter, and the demand for more songs even greater. Artists like Jay-Z and Dr. Dre wanted to make songs with him, The Rapper loved it. Finally, he got the recognition he had longed for so long. Finally, he was good enough. Finally, better than Kygo. From the Rapper's basement, they published song after song, and the fanbase grew with each song that came out. The Rapper had become a star in record time.

As the concert day approached, the Rapper started to get nervous. "What if I mess up? What if my ugly face ruins everything we've worked so hard for?" Manager tried to reassure him, "As an artist, nobody cares about what you look like." With more money than he ever imagined, the Rapper spared no expense for the concert. "When I walk on stage, I want to look like Jesus. I want people to think i am Jesus-beautiful," the Rapper exclaimed. Manager was confused, "Jesus-beautiful?" "Yeah, nobody can hate Jesus," the Rapper replied. "It should be a divine entrance that takes people's breath away. I want to blind them with bright white lights, I'll have long brown hair, and wear a white, transparent tunic." Manageren smiled knowingly, especially at the last part.

As the rapper stood nervously behind the stage, the half-naked and drunken fans covered in neon paint and cocaine had gathered inside the arena, and 125,000 people were waiting in anticipation. Everything was set for what could be one of the greatest concerts in history. "You've come so far, it's just a few steps before you can step into something new and finally overcome your fears," said the Manager.

As the music played, the stage lights grew stronger and stronger, and the fans could barely see what was happening on stage. A biblical "ahh..." spread among the anxious listeners as something holy appeared before them. The rapper stepped forward into the light, with his arms outstretched to the side. With over 40 massive LED screens, the fans finally got to see him. None of the audience could manage to say a single word. It was so quiet that you could hear a spliff hit the ground. The rapper didn't dare open his eyes at first - finally, everyone could see who he was and how he actually looked! He shone his ugliness onto 125,000 people and heard screaming and howling! Wait, screaming and howling...?

He opened his eyes. People ran into each other, towards each other, babies were trampled on while some pulled out their own eyes. Like a microwave heating up food, the molecules in their brains began to boil. The rapper's ugliness was all-consuming and wherever they ran, he radiated his ugliness. One by one, their heads went PUFF. The rapper watched the panic, it was like New Year's Eve fireworks, but there were no pretty colors, just blood and brain matter from thousands of people, including the band. It was too much for them, his ugliness was too unique, too dangerous! It's something that shouldn't be described, it's too damaging to even think about. It's a Pandora's box you shouldn't open.

The rapper stood still and the Manager came out on stage and stood next to him in the light. The Manager looked deep into his eyes and stroked his face. The bright light blocked out all the chaos and it felt like they were in heaven. "You're really Jesus-like," said the Manager. They had never looked at each other like that before. PUFF, then his head exploded too. Covered in the blood and brain matter of his best friend, the rapper walked out of the light. It looked like God had tried to make bolognese sauce out of human brains. That's when the rapper realized he was the best and ugliest rapper alive.

The Cleaning Lady and The Sofa Racist

Ozila always accepted the evening shifts with a grateful heart. Without understanding what the office workers were doing at the offices, she happily cleaned every toilet in the large, anonymous building. She scrubbed the floors and polished the windows so vigorously that her 63-year-old back had started to protest – it was a joyful pain.

After every shift, as she and her colleagues left the office building, she always took a deep breath and admired her workplace with pride. Just a few years ago, she and her daughters clung to a crowded little boat and crossed the sea with the hope of a better life. She was grateful they survived the journey, but the sight of the countless unknowns who perished still haunted her. Those who fell into the sea, those who died of thirst, those who died of hunger, and those who took their own lives before the boat reached land.

She had learned to speak fluent Norwegian after two years. Her daughters Ramla and Paulina had already started studying at school. All three finally felt safe and proudly called themselves Norwegian. Out of nowhere, a man muttered something angry. "Excuse me?" Ozila was shocked. The man stopped and said, "Fucking foreigner. You take our jobs and our money and kill Norwegian culture!" Like a group of elephant mothers, her colleagues surrounded her. "Hey, get out of here!" "What kind of thing is that to say?" Ozila was stunned by the comment, never having heard anything like it before. Shocked to be scolded by her own compatriots, the man angrily replied, "I should get out of here? Really? This is Norway, my country! Can you see my skin color? It's white, can't you see it?! Fuck off back to where you came from." The man was red-eyed and pointed his finger sternly at Ozila. "Get the hell out of here."

As Ozila cooked dinner at home, her thoughts kept playing the scenario over and over in her head. The adrenaline from the day's events still pumped through her veins. It was difficult to shake off the feeling, and her daughters noticed that their mother was absent-minded. The last time they saw her like this was when the city was in ruins and they knew that their family and friends would never return. Hidden and scattered underground, Ozila and her daughters had to take only what they could carry and leave everything behind. She went to bed with a heavy heart that night, unable to shake the feeling that she was a thief. She, of all people, knew what it was like to be robbed of something, to lose everything, and she didn't wish that feeling on anyone.

It didn't take long before Ozila encountered the man again. But this time, he was so drunk that he didn't even register her, or her skin color. Filled with guilt, she decided to catch up to him and apologize for what she had taken. She ran as fast as she could, but the pain in her back was unbearable. With all her might, she tried to yell out to him, but with his new AirPods on full blast, the man could only hear angry and frustrated podcast voices talking about creeping Islamization and immigrants.

"Do you know the name of the man over there?" Two young boys played soccer in front of a worn and old building. They turned and watched the man enter the door. "Oh, you should stay away from him, he's a Sofa Racist," they said. With red cheeks and a beanie that had slipped to the top of his head, they continued kicking the ball back and forth.

"Which of these buttons is his?" Ozila pointed to all the doorbells.

"He's bad news, lady. But if you must know, he lives in the top apartment." Ozila said nothing, just smiled and thought, "Today's youth, they don't know how good they have it." She turned and rang the doorbell.

"Hello?" said the man.

"Hi, my name is Ozila..."

The man interrupted: "I don't have time for this Islamic nonsense, I don't want anything to do with Allah," and hung up.

"Wow, what a jerk," said the boys.

This seemed odd to her, as she wasn't a Muslim, she was a Christian and always wore a cross around her neck. She wrote down his name from the doorbell and walked calmly back to the subway. "Poor man. Imagine not having a job to go to, it's no wonder he's so angry and sad."

The next day, Ozila called her boss. "Are you sure, have you thought this through?" the boss asked. "Yes, this is what I want," she nervously replied. "Good luck." Ozila dialed Sofaracist´s number and nervously pressed the green call button.
"Hello?" "Hi, I'm Ozila, I rang your doorbell yesterday."
"I'm not interested in buying anything."
"I'm sorry, I'm not trying to sell you anything. I'm the cleaning lady you called a thief."

The man thought about all the people he had called a thief. Maybe it was someone at the pub, or on the subway, or at the mall? "Seven years ago, I lost everything. My entire family and my whole life. I know in my heart how painful it is to lose someone you love. I'm sorry I took your job. Work is so important, work makes you happy, work gives life meaning! I don't want to be the reason you feel sad."

"Um, yeah ... well, I'm not that unhappy ... I just ..."
Ozila interrupted, "That's why I talked to my boss. I would like to give my job to you."
"Huh?" Sofaracist replied.
"I don't have much, I work part-time as a cleaning lady in different offices in Oslo. We clean big office spaces, it's heavy

work. Take care of your back. You will get kind colleagues who make you smile every day. That's what I have, and that's what I can give."

With teary eyes, she hung up, afraid that she might lose what she loved most in the world, apart from her daughters. The phone rang, and before the Boss could say hello, Sofaracit started talking. "Hey, I'll take her job, are you organized? 'Cause I don't want to get minimum wage. Workers over 18 years are entitled to receive 16 dollars per hour, I won't take anything less than 200. And about the back... well, I think it's going to be stressful. I'm watching these TV shows from the US. Yeah, got a satellite dish, buddy. On 24/7 Daily Sales, they have self-cleaning equipment. It's almost like magic. Although they advertise it for houses, I think it could also work in an office building. Don't you agree?"

The boss shook his head and asked, "What are you talking about?"
"What am I talking about? Come on, keep up here. I'm talking about improving your cleaning company. And by the way, working hours... It's important. I won't start before 10:00 am."

The boss was clearly annoyed and interrupted, "Well, you can't just decide when to start. We're a staffing agency that provides cleaning services for office spaces. The companies themselves determine when we should clean, and we have to adapt to their needs. Often they don't want us there when they're working, so the shifts start either very early or very late. However, the late shifts are better paid, and many employees earn evening bonuses. There's a big competition for these shifts, and I only assign them to those who have been here the longest. So, in other words, your shifts start around six in the morning"

Sofarascit scratched his head, trying to understand what the boss was saying. "Okay... I see. But can you buy the cleaning equipment from Daily Sales then? I don't want to have back problems like that Ozila lady talked about. And about the pay, I want you to pay me every other week, and the salary must be on my account before 12 pm."

"I think you have misunderstood something here. Pay is disbursed monthly and not every other week, as Social Service does, if I'm not mistaken? Pay also depends on how much you work. If you take fewer shifts, you get less pay. There is no fixed salary since there are no fixed shifts," the boss explained patiently.

"Ehm...Yes, that's true, I'm on Social Service. You don't need to belittle me like that. But...getting paid every month? That could be a problem. I don't want to work more than two to three times a week. And how many vacation days do I get? I usually go to Spain with my pals every year, and I need to afford it."

"Only day shifts, two to three shifts per week...then you can't expect to receive a lot. It won't be more than 700-900 dollars after taxes, I think," the boss responded.

"What the... darn it! What are you talking about? I can't live on that little. How am I supposed to afford drinks at the local pub and still go to Gran Canaria during the summer holidays? Good lord, what is this?! Slavery?!"

"Wait, let me stop you right there. Before we discuss salary, vacation days, and all that, you need to be hired first, and... I don't know what to say, I..."

"You don't need to say anything... I don't want the job. This is a scam! Goodbye." As the man slammed the phone down, he seethed with anger. He scoured his filthy apartment for his iPad, finally uncovering it beneath empty beer cans and cigarette butts. Covered in greasy fingerprints and dirt from 2006, he furiously googled "Cleaning Services in Norway." He devoured article after article, growing more and more incensed at the poor working conditions of these people. Poor folks, poor Ozila, he thought. Although his calculations were entirely incorrect and based solely on her working two to three shifts a week, he was so angry that steam seemed to rise from his ears.

The more he read and thought about it, the angrier he became. He opened the notes on his iPad and resolved to write an article on the working conditions of cleaning services in Norway. The title of the article was: "Cleaning Services: A Slave Trade?" But before he finished writing it, he had already found something else to be angry about—the sugar tax was about to increase.

Meanwhile, the boss called Ozila and said, "The job is yours. He doesn't want it."

"Are you absolutely sure?" she asked.

"One hundred percent," he replied.

Ozila thanked her boss and smiled with joy again. Later that evening, she stood outside the office building, taking a deep breath after her evening shift. Her back still ached, but she didn't care. She was happy with what little she had.

Musti-Man

As Norwegian Knut threw his beer at Musti and shouted, "Fuckin cockroach, there are bloody loads of you everywhere!" his buddies chanted monkey noises and egged him on to continue the disgusting harassment.

Unbeknownst to the drunken and racist gang, God and Gabriel watched the drama unfold. No one could see them, but they could see everyone. They watched as Musti ran behind the asylum center and hid, while the beer flew past him in slow motion, and they munched on popcorn.

"What the hell are they doing?" asked God, stuffing his mouth with more popcorn. Gabriel replied exasperatedly, "You know why they're doing this. Musti is a refugee from Syria. There's a war in Syria, remember? I've told you several times that you need to do something about it."

"Okay, okay, I'll look into it later. But why are they bullying Musti? He hasn't done anything to them?" replied God.

Gabriel: "Ignorance, prejudice, fear... the usual cocktail of human stupidity."
God shrugged, "Well, they're certainly good at that."
Gabriel: "Norwegian Knut is angry because he thinks Musti has come to leech off Norway, take jobs, and destroy Norwegian culture."
God: "How is Musti going to take Knut's job? Musti doesn't speak Norwegian, he hasn't even finished school. Most likely, he'll get a bad job, become depressed, and commit suicide. I don't understand what Knut is so afraid of."

Gabriel: "God... it's always been like this. Refugees come here with nothing, yet they're still a threat to people."

God smiled mischievously: "I'm going to give Musti something."
Gabriel rolled her eyes, knowing that God was probably going to suggest something crazy. Gabriel: "What?"

God: "I'm going to give him the best superpowers, witness it. I've never done this before."
Gabriel: "Whatever you do, just please, don't do anything stupid."

God: "Nope, Abracadabra!"
Gabriel: "Abracadabra? Here we go..."

God: "There you go."
Gabriel: "What did you do now?"

God: "I gave him superpowers that let him switch bodies with racists and take their jobs. Come on, let's tell him!"

Gabriel: "Um, God? How are you going to appear to Musti?"
God: "Maybe I should come as Jesus?"
Gabriel: "Jesus? He's Muslim."
God: "Oh, right. How about Muhammad?"
Gabriel: "Seriously? Muslims don't even know what Muhammad looks like."
God: "Yeah, you're right. Maybe I'll just appear as a light, that's good enough."

Meanwhile, Musti was hiding behind a dumpster, terrified of what the drunk men might do. He couldn't move a muscle as he cried and thought about the sacrifices he had made to come to the safest country in the world. When would it all end? When would he have a life where he wasn't discriminated against, hated, or killed, just for being a regular human being? Suddenly, a small light appeared in front of Musti and he was so shocked that he stared straight into it.

God: «Musti, you're in the presence of God, the Alpha, the Omega. The Creator of everything you see, breathe, and move. I'm here to give you a superpower that will get you out of this shithole.»

Musti was offended. Why did God call the asylum center a shithole? Despite being angry and terrified, he could only manage to say, "Okay?"

God: «Wait, just a okay? Aren't you surprised to see me? Look at me, I'm God, I'm the reason you're alive today!»

Musti: «I was doing fine in Syria. You could have done something about the war, so I wouldn't have had to flee to this shithole.»

Gabriel understood that it had to intervene before God got angry and did something stupid. Gabriel revealed itself as it was, a majestic creature.

Gabriel: «Musti. Show some respect for God Almighty.» With silky white hair, skin that shimmered in all the colors of the rainbow, and wings so large they could hide ten refugees under each wing, Musti stared in horror at the angel.

God was feeling insecure as usual. "Why do people always get so excited when they see angels, but not when they see me? Are angels cooler than G-O-D?!"

Musti stood frozen, too scared to answer. God sighed, realizing he was already over this conversation. "Musti, your superpowers are that you can take the jobs of racists, and as an added bonus, you can understand and speak every language in the world. Use these powers to give them nightmares."

And just like that, God and Garbriel disappeared into thin air, leaving Musti standing there wondering if he had just imagined the whole thing.

Gabriel spoke up, "You forgot to mention the downside of these superpowers and the fact that they will make him enemies."

God retorted, "Well, he thought you were way cooler than me, so he'll figure it out for himself." Gabriel didn't know what to say, this was just classic God. Always jealous and quick to anger. Maybe that was why the world was going to hell.

Shocked and scared, Musti looked around, had he drunk enough water today? Were the drunk racists still there? He ran into the asylum center and hoped with all his might that everyone was gone. He sat around the dining table with the other refugees. In the short time he had been there, he saw these people as his extended family. With their own problems and traumas, they now sat gratefully under the same roof and ate in peace. Astrid volunteered at the asylum center and came smiling into the dining room. In her hands, she held a large tray of evening snacks, bread with cheese and jam. Musti couldn't understand how this country could call this proper food. He was so tired of the dry and tasteless bread.

Astrid: "Hey Musti! It's great that you made it for dinner! I know this isn't your favorite food, but I saved a slice of apricot jam for you."

Musti replied without thinking: "Thanks, I appreciate it, Astrid." Astrid was completely blank-faced. She had never heard him manage to complete a whole sentence, and especially not in perfect Norwegian.

Astrid: "Musti! You can speak Norwegian!"
Musti: "Huh? Do you understand what I'm saying?"
Astrid: "Yes, this is amazing!"
Musti: "Right, it's great, I have to go, good night."

Musti grabbed his sandwich and ran into his bedroom. He paced frantically in front of the small and worn-out cot. Has he really met God? Was there a light at the end of the tunnel?

Superpower: "Hey hey hey, calm down now, little man, your journey has only just begun."
Musti: "Huh? Hello? Who's there?"
Superpower: "It's me, your good friend who's going to help you get out of this shithole."
Musti: "Shithole? Where are you? Show yourself, you devil."
Superpower: "Oh dear, now you need to calm down. Devil? He could never create such a great superpower."
Musti: "Where are you?!"
Superpower: "I'm inside your head, buddy! Right between your ears, deep inside your brain, or I can go anywhere. Go to the mirror, and you'll see for yourself!"
Musti rushed to the bathroom and looked at himself in the mirror.
Musti: "So, where are you?"

Superpower: "Can't you see me? Look closer..."

Musti pressed his face against the mirror, so close that the condensation appeared and disappeared with his breath.

Superpower: "Closer..."
Musti: "I can't get any closer, where the hell are you?"
Superpower: "Look at the small vein in your left eye. Right now, I'm flowing through it, dancing my way around..."

Musti looked at his left eye and saw the little vein pulsing in a familiar rhythm.

Superpower: "Hey there, Musti, it's nice to meet you! I'm Superpower, and we're going to have a blast together. Let's start with that Norwegian guy, Knut. He's going to get what's coming to him for everything he did to you!"
Musti: "What do you mean, get what's coming to him?"

Superpower: "Oh, you know, some payback. But let's leave that for tomorrow. Right now, I'm going to check out some of your old memories. Amina was so cute, wasn't she? Catch you later!"

Musti shouted in panic, "Hey, those are private memories! Don't go there! Superpower, are you there? Superpower!!" The blood vessel in his left eye had stiffened, and Musti slammed his fist on the sink in frustration. Nobody was going to mess with the best and most beautiful memories he had of his true love. He walked out of the bathroom and collapsed into bed. Was he just arguing with a blood vessel in his left eye? Was he going crazy? With a thousand chaotic thoughts racing through his mind, he finally lowered his head onto the pillow and closed his eyes. And that's when he dreamed…

Musti kicked down door after door, searching for Norske Knut. Suddenly, he found himself standing face to face with Norske Knut in a warehouse. In the next moment, Musti was back at the asylum center, staring at himself in the mirror. He had become Norske Knut… Terrified, he tried to peel off his face, but it was stuck.

Musti woke up drenched in sweat and ran into the bathroom to look at himself in the mirror. He was still himself! Relieved that he hadn't turned into a disgusting racist with yellow teeth, he stepped into the shower.

Superpower: "Ahh, the water is freezing cold!"
Musti: "Is that you, God?"
Superpower: "No. It's me, Superpower… Today we have a job to do, you idiot. So get out of this icy water and put on some clothes."
Three hours later, Musti stood in front of a large and anonymous warehouse.
Musti: "I'm not so sure I want to do this anymore…"
Superpower: "Don't be a coward now, Musti. Don't you remember what he did to you yesterday? Let's give him a proper lesson!"

Musti: "Treat others the way you want to be treated."

Superpower: "Don't give me that god stuff. Go in, or I'll delete Amina from your memory."

Musti: "You wouldn't dare..."

Superpower: "Try me."

Musti: "Fine."

Superpower: "Hallelujah! Go into the bathroom, and you'll see how real godly stuff works!"

Reluctantly, Musti walked into the warehouse and found a handicap bathroom. He looked seriously into the mirror.

Superpower: "Okay, now I want you to stick your index finger as far into your ear as possible."

Musti looked at his finger and reluctantly complied. "Okay, now what?" He felt a small pulsation at the very end of his fingertip.

Superpower: "High five!"

Musti rolled his eyes. "I didn't come here to be bullied by you. Just tell me what to do or I'm out."

Superpower: "We'll have to work on your sense of humor. But fine. Spin around and count to three."

Musti spun around three times and counted aloud. When he finished, he looked at himself in the mirror. He had become Norske Knut! "Oh my god, this can't be possible!"

Superpower: "My friend, I can turn you into any racist in the world. And no, you won't be stuck as that jerk forever. You're going to take his job, and he'll experience your life. He'll feel how scary and difficult it is to be a foreigner, and how much worse it gets when you're not met with respect."

Musti nervously looked around the lunchroom filled with big white men in blue work uniforms just like him. He wasn't sure he could pull off being Norske Knut without getting caught.

Musti: "What if they see through me?"
Superpower: "Can't you just for once stop overthinking?"
With a deep breath, Musti kicked open the door and nervously looked around the room. Suddenly, all the big white men burst out laughing.

Buddy 1: "Knut...you gotta stop drinking so much."
Relieved, Musti sat down with his new job buddies.
Buddy 2: "Yeah, you're one of a kind. Last weekend at the company party, you were dancing on the table, flirting with Kari, and then you went off on that poor immigrant!"
Musti: "Haha, maybe I had a few too many Piña Coladas."

Superpower was ecstatic, "Now you're getting the hang of it! You've got nothing to lose, so let's teach this Norske Knut a lesson." Musti discreetly stuck his finger in his ear.

Superpower shouted, "High five!" Musti put on Norwegian Knut's headset and cranked up *"Eye of the Tiger."* He was ready. He stormed into the warehouse and knocked over an entire shelf of "fragile" glass, slapped Kari's butt, and to top it off, left a poop-stained handkerchief in Norwegian Knut's locker - his confidence in his superpower growing with each passing minute. "We can do even better. The next racist will be filthy rich," said Musti as he left the warehouse. He stopped and spotted a familiar figure. It was Norwegian Knut, who was trapped in a foreigner's body.

Norwegian Knut stuttered, "I job, no, no, I mean I work. No... listen to me." Norske Knut's worst nightmare had come true - a foreigner had actually taken his job. Musti couldn't help but smile. Norwegian Knut pointed at Musti and said, "Look!! Foreigner, I Norwegian. He, yes, that's my job," but the boss was fed up.

Boss: "Do you know who this is, Knut?"
Musti: "Never seen him before." Musti arrogantly winked and bumped into Norwegian Knut as he walked past the desperate foreigner. "Fucking kebab face." In heaven, Gabriel sat with a "Team Musti" hat on his head and closely followed the drama that unfolded. "Ouch, that stings! 1-0 to Musti! But hey, God, don't you think this superpower will go to his head? Shouldn't we inform him about the consequences of switching bodies with racists?"

God waved Gabriel off with his hand. He was too busy watching Michael Jordan's new documentary and talking on the phone with him so that Michael himself could confirm what was true and what was not. Musti felt invincible! On his way home, when no one could see him, he did a victory dance and spun around. Poof, and Musti was back.

Superpower: "My friend, I take my hat off to you. That was legendary!"

Back at the asylum center, Musti was still pumped with adrenaline. He was God's chosen one, and he was going to teach these racists a lesson. He needed to find more racists, and preferably rich ones! Musti picked up his phone and googled "Norwegian racists." There were so many of them. In the comment section of the news alone, there were racists that deserved a lesson. But there was one story that made a strong impression. Fatima from Grorud had written a post where she explained in detail how a racist who didn't like her hijab had spit in her face. The racist had a name, Steve, and Fatima didn't hide what he did for a living, namely a stockbroker. Three quick searches later, Musti knew exactly who Rich Steve was and where he worked.

Musti: "Superpower? What do you say, should we give Rich Steve a big lesson?"

Superpower: "Oh, we definitely should! But let's do it tomorrow. I have a date with Amina behind a tree on a warm summer night. I think it's going to be hot. See you later!"

Musti: "No... ahh, that's private."

Musti wanted to tell Astrid and everyone at the asylum center what he had done today. He had stood up for himself and made sure there was one less racist in the world. He was so happy! But he knew nobody would believe him. They would probably send a worried letter that could ruin his chances of getting a residency permit. No, he couldn't tell anyone. Musti lay down in bed, his head filled with thousands of questions he would never get answers to. His head sank into the pillow, his eyes closed, and that's when he dreamed…

Musti is back! He eagerly kicks down door after door until he suddenly finds himself in a large, empty office. He looks down at his body, dressed in a tight Superman-like suit. His muscles have become significantly larger, and on his big, hairy chest is a large "M". An M for Musti, Musti the man, Musti-Man! In the same moment, Rich Steve appears. Musti smiles confidently and meets his gaze.

Superpower: "Good morning, Musti! Are you ready for new adventures?"
Musti: "Musti-Man."
Superpower: "Musti-Man?"
Musti: "All superheroes have a superhero name. Mine is Musti-Man."
Superpower: "I love the style. So, Musti-Man, are you ready to cook this potato and mash him into the world's tastiest and least racist mashed potatoes?"
Musti: "Let's do this!" And he stuck his finger in his ear.
Superpower: "High five!"

A few hours later, Musti stood in front of a large and anonymous office building. He took a deep breath and went in. Just like the day before, he found a toilet and spun around while counting to three. When Musti saw himself in the mirror, he had become Rich Steve.

Superpower: "Poor guy, he should never have messed with Fatima. You can do this, Musti-Man!"

Musti-Man adjusted his tie and strutted out of the restroom with the confidence of a superhero. The office was buzzing with activity as people shouted and ran around. Suddenly, an employee called out, "Steve! What are we doing here?" and pointed to a sheet of paper covered in numbers and graphs.

Musti-Man: "Sell."
Employee: "Are you sure? What about this one?"
Musti-Man: "Sell!"

Musti clapped his hands.

Musti-Man: "Today, you're going to sell everything this company owns. I don't care how you do it, just get it done. And, by the way, you're all fired."
The entire office came to a standstill.
Musti-Man: "Now!"
Musti walked into the office and sat down in a massive leather chair. A nervous assistant entered and could barely maintain eye contact.
Assistent: "Someone is here to see you..."
Musti-Man interrupts: "I need to open a bank account. You

will do this and deposit 10 million, and never, ever speak of this again. Understand?"

Assistent: "Okay, what about your father?"

Musti-Man: "No, he definitely should not know about this."

Assistent: "Okay, but there's..."

Musti-Man: "And you'll have that done within the hour."

Assistent: "THERE'S SOMEONE OUTSIDE WHO WANTS TO TALK TO YOU! He's been pestering us since we opened. We didn't dare let him in, he's waiting for you at the reception."

Musti recognized the man and smiled, "Thank you, you can go now."

God exclaimed, "Look here, look here, Musti is learning quickly! Gabriel go and get some more salt. This popcorn tastes like nothing."

Gabriel: "... It's Musti-Man."

Musti went down and met another desperate foreigner-Musti. Rich Steve was angry and shouted loudly, "No! Why? No, my account, my job. My life!" Musti took out his phone and started a live stream on Facebook. Musti-Man: "Yuck, you smell like garlic. Don't you brush your teeth?" Rich Steve was speechless. The powerful voice had disappeared, and he didn't know what to say. Musti continued, "So you think you can come here and get a job, looking like that? Those clothes must be burned because they're probably infested with pests." Rich Steve looked like a wounded bully victim - he was so small that an ant could have carried him on its shoulders. Musti spat on him and laughed out loud, "fucking immigrant."

Then he turned the phone towards himself and said, "My name is Steve, and I'm a fucking racist. I hate brown people, I hate all immigrants!" On the other side of town, Rich Richard was stunned by the drama unfolding on Facebook. His son had exposed them and ruined everything. Forty years ago, a dark shadow appeared in front of him and gave him the superpower of racial division, enabling him to create fear and hatred among all nationalities. With the Norwegian government wrapped around his little finger, he had become filthy rich. Shocked, he watched the life he had sold his soul for crumble away.

Superpower: "I tip my hat to you. That was savage!"

Musti-Man: "I didn't know I had it in me. Oh my god, ten million! Imagine what we can do with all that money!"
Musti called the assistant back in.
Musti-Man: "Are all the funds transferred?"
Assistant: "Yes... Are you really a racist?"
Musti-Man: "Of course I am! Now, I want you to donate all the money to this asylum center. You will say that the money is only to be used for this: renovation of common areas, prayer rooms for all religions, botanical garden, library, TV and PlayStation 5 in every bedroom, a permanent Norwegian teacher, and most importantly, a damn big hot water tank."
Assistant: "Okay... So you're a racist, but you want these foreigners to be well taken care of?"
Musti-Man: "Did I ask for your permission?"
Assistant: "No, no! I'll take care of it!"

Superpower: "Your job is done. We have to leave now!"

Musti exited the office and saw panic and hatred in his colleagues' eyes. He understood them well, considering all he had caused in the last hour. He ran to the elevator, walked out of the office building, and shouted a loud "YESSS!" before spinning around and turning back to his old self.

Rich Steve came home crying to Rich Richard, trying his best to explain what had happened. Someone had taken over his body! And he had become an immigrant! Rich Steve took out a note he had found in the pants pocket of the terrible, soon-to-be-dead rat: *"Hey, Rich Steve! I, Musti-Man, have taken over your body, and you can't do a damn thing about it. You will now live in this immigrant body until you have learned your lesson, you fucking racist. Enjoy."*

Rich Richard looked shocked at the note. Were there others with superpowers like him? In his office, in his large palace at the outermost part of Bygdøy, he pressed a red button hidden under the penis of a naked sculpture of his ex-wife. The floor opened, and they headed down. Rich Richard had had many years to prepare, and judgment day had arrived. Now he would train his son to take over for him, and with a specially designed superhero suit with a big "R" on his chest, Rich Steve would become Rase-Man - the superhero who would restore order. The first step was to investigate this asylum center, which was now a five-star hotel. Musti was not aware that his biggest enemy was just around the corner.

Far below the ground, the Devil ate burnt popcorn drenched in sugar - finally, his investment paid off. God's little stunt couldn't compare to what the Devil had caused.

The Devil called God.

"What do you want now? Do you want me to turn up the heat?" asked God as he laughed at himself. Gabriel rolled his eyes and realized who was on the other end of the phone.

"Musti-Man, huh... an exciting type. But have you heard of Rase-Man?" asked the Devil.

"Rase-Man?" replied God. The Devil hung up before God could respond and did a victory dance.

If Grannies Ruled the World

If grannies ruled the world, warfare would be a thing of the past. However, what we would have instead are endless discussions with tiny coffee breaks sprinkled in. If there was too much to chat about, the solution would be to sleep on it. And if disagreements persisted, further discussions would take place at a "bring-your-own-cat-or-dog" dinner party.

Countless hours have been spent deliberating how to make the world a better place. Behold, the resolutions:

1. Everyone must own a cat or dog. *(Wishing for more pets is allowed, but only at Christmas. If you've been good and kind, you might just find a furry little creature in your next stocking.)*

2. Respect thy neighbor's lawn. Treading on someone else's

turf, especially if there's a **"keep off the grass"** sign, is strictly forbidden. Break this rule, and we'll confiscate one of your cats. *(Don't worry, no kitties will be harmed; we'll just give it to someone who respects other people's lawns.)*

3. Knitting is an essential life skill, and everyone must learn it.

4. Lifetime phone subscriptions for all – after all, chit-chatting for hours on end is perfectly normal.

5. Everyone must embark on at least one cruise in their lifetime.

6. Bingo halls are mandatory in every neighborhood, and bringing your cat or dog is permitted.

7. Host a dinner party for one another at least once a month, and feel free to bring your furry friends.

8. All old people will receive a never-ending Visa card, exclusively for staying at insanely expensive hotels, indulging in exotic cuisine, and visiting the dream destinations of their childhood.

Rapewomen

Sara had pursued her idol for as long as she could remember, yet it was almost disheartening that she had never found her. For it was none other than RapeWoman who discovered Sara. Sara was a renowned YouTuber, who, on a weekly basis, engaged her audience in discussions on equality, feminism, and racism. But it wasn't until she released the video, "No means NO," that her channel gained international recognition and amassed millions of streams. She had cracked the code, managing to unite people of diverse beliefs, ethnicities, and genders in profound and reflective conversations – her platform was the haven one would visit when they yearned to be heard.

In recent years, RapeWoman had become a heated and highly debated topic. For women, she was a symbol of freedom, while for men, a chilling and menacing figure. Who was she? Why did she do what she did? Was it ethically sound? Rumors of RapeWoman's true identity had originated in India, but Sara wasn't entirely convinced by the conspiracy theory that RapeWoman was the Hindu goddess Kali – the bloodthirsty and uncontrollable deity who eradicated evil to protect the innocent. The first woman who took the law into her own hands. Sara sat, tense with anticipation, in the bar at The Thief. The camera was ready, and in fear of forgetting to press record, she had already begun filming. RapeWoman was twenty minutes late. Concerned she might exhaust the memory card before RapeWoman arrived, she pressed pause and checked her phone. No missed calls. Sara was always irritated when the person who proposed the time and place was late. She glanced at her phone's background, a poorly sketched police sketch of RapeWoman – *it could have been anyone.* Frustrated, she scanned the room for anyone. At that very moment, an elegant woman entered the bar. Her skin was a rich, chocolate hue, and her curly hair was tightly pulled back in a ponytail. Her clothes clung to her form. Her hips, her backside, her breasts – the entire woman was striking. The epitome of perfection. She smiled confidently, extending her hand, "Hello, Sara." Sara's entire body trembled with excitement. At last, she was here. The air felt electric. Sara could not wait a second longer and turned the camera back on. "Are you truly Kali, the goddess of a thousand faces?"

At that very moment, eight women at the four nearest tables turn to face Sara. "I am the ultimate mother, the mother of all power. I am here and simultaneously a hundred other places. In the present, the past, and the future," Kali declares as the women calmly turn back.

RapeWoman, Kali, had been present all along. Sara glances nervously around the bar, wondering if any of the people are real – had she bitten off more than she could chew? Kali reassuringly takes Sara's hand. "My friend, there is nothing to fear. Although I am the destroyer of evil, wild, ugly, and merciless, I have not lost my maternal role. I am as loving as I am dangerous. You have nothing to fear. As a young girl, you dreamed of living in a world without rape. I am here to fulfill your dream."

Kali's hand is warm, and Sara feels a loving presence she remembers from her own mother when she was little, nestled in her lap. She takes a deep breath, "Why now?"

Kali zones out, her gaze fixed emptily on the glass before her, a worried crease forming between her eyes. She blinks, and she's back. "I am your mother, and I feel all your pain at once," she regains her composure, "I don't know why I returned here, why now. The cosmos is a vast network of chaos, perfectly intertwined. The world has not become a better place, and I cannot accept that."

"What can I do to help?" asks Sara.
"I want you to convey my message, my love and relentlessness.

Tell the world that I do not tolerate rape, and that one will be punished for it. I have been here for a long time, watching your world and seeing what transpires. When women are subjected to sexual assault, many do not believe them. Who decides what happened, if not the victim themselves?"

"Yes... The few, strong women who come forward are not always taken seriously. Did she wear too much makeup? What was she wearing? Did she do something that led to the assault? Was she too drunk? Imagine how many never dare to speak up... It's utterly dreadful. If only there were a way to prove an assault took place," Sara says supportively. "For words against words are nearly impossible to prove, and then it's easier to say it never happened."

"I see women who dare not leave their homes after the sun has set, some even afraid to leave their rooms. They call friends when walking in unsafe neighborhoods, saying, 'Will you talk to me? It's dark and scary outside.' Why is it scary, Sara?" Kali inquires.

Sara says nothing, for the answer is obvious. Kali is the realist who sees the world as it is, a world others acknowledge but dare not act upon. It's appalling. Kali continues: "It's frightening, Sara, because you don't want a perverse man to exploit you with his filthy organ. You call a friend so they can alert the police if something actually happens. Then the question is, will the police arrive in time? Don't you want to live in a world where you don't have to worry? Don't you want to live in a world where your daughter knows nothing of rape?"

"Yes, but is it possible?"

"That's why I'm here, I will punish the men who commit these acts. Those who get off lightly, those who think only of themselves. They shall all meet my Penis Cutter and never again perform such a deed." Sara had heard of the Penis Cutter, the whole world had heard of the Penis Cutter. Sinister tales recounted its brutal attributes, but no one had come forward to confirm what was true or false – no one would admit to having raped someone. Thus, the Penis Cutter remained a mystery, instilling fear and desperation among men worldwide. Sara inquires further: "How does the Penis Cutter work?"

"If I desire, I can sever a man's penis if he rapes me. It responds to stress signals from my body and defends me if I am attacked. At this very moment, four versions of me have cut off the penises of four men in India. They thought they could exploit women from a lower caste. Now they have learned that rape cannot be justified," Kali replies.

"That's quite extreme. At the same time, it's quite extreme to rape someone. But how do you know the men will learn, will you be here forever?" Sara follows up. "My time here is nearing its end; I must move on. Together with a trusted group of scientists, we have researched my blood and developed a hormonal IUD for all women on Earth. Now you can reclaim nightlife, dark streets, and your sexuality, becoming equal to men." Sara can't believe what she hears; it seems too good to be true. "So, can I become like you? A god?" With a sly smile, Kali responds: "Not quite, but you'll borrow one of my abilities. In simple terms, my blood will protect you and all other women in the world."

"But how do you know that we women won't misuse the hormonal IUD or cut it off accidentally?"

"If only it were that simple. My blood cannot be deceived; it knows when it's under attack and acts accordingly. Just as women have the right to engage in sexual activity without fear for their lives, so do men. The hormonal IUD ensures that both parties must give consent before the act begins. This is where your role comes in, Sara. I am not unjust, but I am relentless. Rape must not occur, and this message you shall convey to all women and men on this small, blue planet."

Kali gazes seriously into her eyes. For Sara, it feels as if Kali is peering directly into her soul, evaluating her deepest thoughts and emotions. Once again, Kali blinks, and she returns. "My dear child, you are so beautiful and strong, both inside and out. You shall spread my word."

A middle-aged man enters the room and takes a seat at a table in the back of the establishment.

"Now, I shall meet a sadistic man who has violated far too

many women. With physical, psychological, and financial power, he escapes each time, the poor women never standing a chance against him. Money and power hold no sway over me, and he shall pay for all the souls he has harmed." Kali hands Sara an earpiece and a hotel key card. "So you can hear everything. If you're brave enough, you may come and watch as I take his manhood."

Kali rises and approaches the man, planting a kiss on his cheek. Sara listens intently to their conversation. Kali is engaged, laughing at the right moments and allowing him to boast of his grand and insignificant conquests. It is clear that this night is not about Kali. Sara feels she should run and shout about who she is, attempting to save this man. But she doesn't.

The man signals a waiter and asks her to charge the bill to his room. He takes Kali by the hand and leads her to the elevator. They ascend to the penthouse suite. Sara hastily packs her camera equipment and follows them. Inside the room, she hears panting and gasping. "This is moving too fast, I don't want to..." "Calm down, my girl, we're just going to have some fun, no need to make a fuss now."

Sara stands outside the door, itching to kick it down and sever his manhood herself. How could he act this way? Startled, she hears the sound of fabric tearing. "I don't want to, stop... Stop!" Kali screams before silence falls. It sounds as if he's covering her mouth with his hand. Suddenly, a man's scream and a woman's laughter erupt from within the room.

Sara pulls the key card from her jacket pocket and rushes in.

There, she finds the man nearly unconscious on the floor, clutching his crotch. He doesn't stop bleeding, blood spurting uncontrollably in every direction. In shock, Sara freezes, unsure of what to say or where to turn. Kali rises, the blood of the now penis-less man dripping down her naked body. Her eyes turn red, a third eye appears on her forehead, and she approaches Sara. Two arms sprout from her ribs – Kali is in her full form.

"Now I leave behind a world striving to find balance, a world where consent shall be inherent, a world where potential rapists must ponder: could she have a Penis Cutter? Is rape worth losing one's manhood?" Sara is appalled. "What the hell?! The Penis Cutter is a deadly weapon, haven't you considered that?" Kali looks down at the man who has ceased to breathe, bled to death. Sara continues, "When you sever an erect penis, wouldn't their bodies just pump out blood and the rapist die rapidly?"

"Yes, but if they receive immediate medical help, they might survive," replies Kali. The once confident goddess suddenly grows uncomfortable. "Besides, it's still addressing the issue of rape. Do you think rapists are prepared to sacrifice their lives? They likely wouldn't want to live without their penises anyway!" It seems as if she felt she'd redeemed herself a bit, but the atmosphere in the room was still not to her liking. Sara hesitates. "So, all those who have lost their penises so far have also died? Is that why no one has shared their story?"
Kali suddenly becomes eager to leave.

"Here I've given you an incredible gift in the fight against rape, and you're only finding problems?! If it's that important, you'll have to find a solution yourselves! At least I've given you the Penis Cutter; use it as you wish. I must go now, farewell, Sara!" concludes Kali before vanishing into thin air. Kali, the original woman, created by nature herself. Sara´s role model.

F*** MY BRAIN!

"The Universe is expanding 5% to 9% faster than previously thought..." – NASA and ESA, June 2016.

Oceans make up 71% of Earth's surface, but we've only explored about 5%. Does that mean mermaids might not be a myth after all? Even though we're taking up more and more of Earth's surface, there are still vast areas we haven't discovered. Like, what viruses and parasites are hiding beneath the permafrost? But I'm not sure I even want to know. Maybe we should focus more on overpopulation and pollution and actually find sustainable solutions. Or just do like Elon Musk and admit that Earth is a lost cause and move to Mars?

Technology is growing at such an intense pace that I wouldn't be surprised if it becomes a reality. We love to gaze up at the stars and wonder if there's life out there. The Universe is infinite and expanding faster than ever, but what does that mean for us, and what exactly is the Universe expanding into?

The Hubble Space Telescope was launched into space on April 24, 1990. Its sole mission? To stare at a single black spot in the cosmos. Scientists didn't know what was there, but they took a chance. They had it gaze at the same spot for ten days, not knowing what they'd find. Behold, they discovered 50,000 galaxies in that black spot. I wonder what would happen if I stared into my significant other's black pupils for ten days straight. Would I uncover 50,000 more galaxies?

The Universe keeps growing, stars are born, and stars die. When a star meets its end, it can create a supernova explosion, which in turn can form a black hole that gobbles up everything in its path. With every passing second, there's even more we don't know about the Universe. It's a thrilling, mysterious place for humans—somewhere we can't venture without protection from a thousand deadly things. There are so many dangers out there that we could perish in an instant. I could meet my demise at this very moment of writing. Good thing I exercise four times a week, get enough sleep, meditate, and avoid smoking, drinking, and fatty foods. But, man, I'm getting tired of all these rules. What happened to just living?

Imagine you were a tiny organism trapped in a droplet of water, so minuscule that you're invisible to the naked eye. You'd probably have no clue how small and insignificant you are compared to the vast and mysterious ocean—an ocean teeming with life, possibly even filled with other organisms you've never seen before. To me, we humans are that tiny organism, except we know there's something bigger out there; we just have no idea about its magnitude. So we build spaceships that can take us into the unknown, perhaps to other galaxies, in search of the meaning of our existence. Because we humans are doomed to believe in something. Who is God? Did they create everything? Why can't God be a woman?

Must we believe in God?

If you don't believe in anything, you're an atheist. But even an atheist must believe in something, be it the Big Bang, aliens, or whatever else. No matter what anyone says, we're bound to believe in something. What if this thing we're fated to believe in is an actual person we're living inside? What if we're an organism spreading like cancer, eventually killing that person with pollution, garbage, and selfish souls? Are they aware they have cancer? Is that why supernovas happen? Are the doctors of the cancer-stricken universe-human killing us, the cancer, with massive radiation treatments? If that's the case, what kind of cancer would we be? F*** MY BRAIN!!!

When Rings Collide

Olav was a boy who enjoyed his own company. He never felt lonely; that's just how Olav was. He found comfort in the small objects he made in his room, and he was particularly proud of the penis ring he crafted—a ring with a tiny penis on top. As he looked at the ring, Olav thought, "Now I'm going to bang everyone I see," and laughed at the idea.

Olav dashed out of his room and saw his mother's friend drinking coffee at the kitchen table. He put the ring on and tapped her shoulder with it. His mother saw this and asked, "What are you doing, Olav?" Olav thought, "Yuck, I can't bang mom's friends." Without answering, he ran out the door and saw some neighborhood boys.

Olav calmly walked up to one of the boys, tapped his shoulder with the penis ring, and laughed. The boy turned to Olav and asked, "What the hell are you doing?" Olav laughed and said, "Haha... You just got banged." The boy's friends began to laugh because it was pretty stupid, but also kind of brilliant. Eventually, everyone started laughing at Olav's antics, which were indeed absurd. Olav continued his mission, entering a store and banging everyone inside.

He then proceeded to bang everyone in the town square and everyone in the parking lot. Olav enjoyed banging outdoors because it was easy to escape if someone saw him. However, he preferred banging behind a car so that no one could watch.

Banging so many people in one day wore Olav out, so he decided to take breaks occasionally. His mother had a chat with him and said, "You can bang as many people as you want, but only after school and after you've done your homework." So, after finishing his homework, Olav went out and banged as many people as he could. He never got tired of banging, but he did grow bored of banging the same people. It wasn't exciting anymore. He had never met someone he loved to bang or actually wanted to bang again.

One day, Olav decided to take the bus out of his area to meet new people he could bang. He headed towards the mall where the cool, older kids from 9th grade hung out. There, he spotted something he had never seen before—someone he couldn't take his eyes off, someone he genuinely wanted to bang. Olav decided to follow her, but she did something oddly familiar. She went up to people, touched their backs, shoulders, or faces, and then ran away. Was she doing what he thought she was doing? Was she banging people too?

Her name was Ruth, and she was like Olav. While Olav had made a penis ring, Ruth had created a vagina ring. Ruth also loved running around and banging people, though not as often as Olav. Suddenly, Ruth spotted Olav and his ring. On opposite sides of the street, they stood and stared at each other. A light breeze sent an old newspaper dancing gently between them. Bang! Olav dropped his backpack and began banging as many people as he could, with Ruth following close behind, always a few steps back. Together, they ran around the mall banging everyone in sight. Once everyone had been banged, they met in the middle and stared at each other. Olav aimed his penis ring at Ruth, and she aimed her vagina ring at Olav.

They slowly moved towards each other, Olav's penis ring gradually entering Ruth's vagina ring. Ruth's vagina ring fit perfectly around his penis ring. They gazed into each other's eyes, and there in the mall, they sat banging each other with their rings. That's how they met, and from that day on, they stopped banging others and only banged each other.

Horses Before Cars

One late evening, a young horse strolls casually into the stable. The horse closes the gate and stands next to an older horse.

Older Horse: "Did you say it exactly as we rehearsed?"
Young Horse: "Yes, I believe it was word for word."

Older Horse: "It's crucial, it's about our species' future. I need to know precisely what you said, if you said it in the right order, and if you got him to write down the invention."

Young Horse: "I told him about the two-stroke gasoline engine and reminded him about the speed control system, spark plug, carburetor, clutch, gears, water radiator, and ignition by sparks to the battery. I explained all the mathematical calculations and repeated everything twice. He wrote it all down."

Older Horse: "That's good, that's good! Did anyone else discover you?"

Young Horse: "No, if anyone approached, I stomped my foot and made lots of strange horse noises."
Older Horse: "Well done. Was he not surprised or scared when you started speaking the human language?"

Young Horse: "Not really. His father, grandfather, and great-grandfather had apparently told the weirdest stories about talking horses. Until he met me, he thought it was just a bad joke."
Older Horse: "That's good, my son, this will change everything. Now we can get rid of these meat-eating creatures on our backs, and we won't have to do all the heavy farm work for them! Once they get this invention working, they'll finally leave us alone, and we can run free and wild into the forest again."

Young Horse: "But, grandpa, if you're so wise, why couldn't you just talk to him?"
Older Horse: "I'm the one with the knowledge, my son. We've tried this many times. Every time a brave horse starts talking to a human about the automobile, they start screaming and grab their shotgun to blast us to pieces."

Young Horse: "So, this was a successful attempt?"
Older Horse: "Are you lying on the floor with your brains splattered all over? No, then I would say it was a successful attempt."

Young Horse: "How many times have we tried this?"
Older Horse: "Far too many times, my son, far too many times.
Now, humans are coming! Stand still and make horse noises."
Karl Benz: "I swear, that horse talked to me! Hey, horse! Tell
me what you told me last night!"

———————————————

Chapter 2

One Brain Cell

Everyday-Tom and the Influencer

Tom gazes out over the water, as he does every morning, hoping to catch sight of a boat or something else that could rescue them. It's been over two weeks, and the only thing he's seen is the sun rising in the east and setting in the west. He doesn't know where they are or what has happened. Everything went dark when the storm hit, and everything was in ruins when he woke up on this deserted island with the Influencer. As the days have passed, he's realized the gravity of the situation. Whatever has happened, he's going to use all his knowledge from boy-scouting and life skills to survive.

"OH MY GOD," shrieks the Influencer, discovering a new pimple on her chin – the combination of humid air and sweat hasn't been kind to her skin. Tom is fascinated by this girl; he's heard of Influencers and seen them on TV and social media – a strange and new breed of humans.

Once, he saw a Chinese influencer trying to eat a live octopus, but it got stuck to her face. As she tried to tear it off, it took some of her skin with it. It might sound very extreme, but it wasn't. It was just a baby-wound. For the rest of the video, she sat there crying in front of the camera, saying, "Look what it did to me! Oh... now my skin is ruined!" But, haha... what did she think would happen? The octopus was just defending itself. Or he heard one of those reality show participants say on TV, "I don't use condoms; I can tell if girls have STDs." Huh? How do you do that? Can you share this information with the rest of us so we can avoid STDs too? Or the most famous story Tom remembered: A woman who used a live lobster as a dildo in a bathtub. The lobster was alive when she supposedly used it, and somehow, she managed to light a lighter on it underwater. When it boiled, it went wild and gave her pleasure. Rumor has it she had a stomach ache the next day and gave birth to a bunch of shrimp babies.

Tom chuckles, giving birth to shrimp... karma, bitch... He had lost himself in his thoughts while he stood there, blankly staring and daydreaming out at the sea. He shakes his head to snap back to the harsh and painful reality. "I have to try to cheer her up, no matter how hard it is." Now, Tom had reached his limit; his patience was spent, and he was fed up with doing everything by himself.

"Why don't you join me today, and I can teach you how to fish?" says Tom, forcing a smile.
"Oh! That sounds like so much fun! But... Umm... Oh, my

stomach hurts. There's been so much fish lately…" Tom takes a deep breath; "it's the only food I've been able to find. If we're going to survive, we have to eat something." The Influencer rolls her eyes. "Come on, it'll be fun! I promise!" She clutches her stomach, "Oh, I don't think it's the fish that's causing my stomach ache. Aunt Flo is just around the corner!" She spreads her legs in front of Tom and looks at the crotch of her shorts. "Any moment now." Tom slowly backs away, angry at the possibility of being lied to right in his face and scared that it might actually be true.

The Influencer pulls out her iPhone and snaps a photo of their surroundings, with Tom in the background, his back turned, casting a homemade fishing line made of shoelaces and tampon strings.

INSTAGRAM POST
"Two weeks u guys… Still going strong! Somebody should consider getting a wax though…"
#Mylife #Boring #Hairybackproblems

A message pops up from JulieTheSurvivor: "I feel you, girl. Still stuck somewhere myself. OMG, there's sand everywhere! #mylife. #friends-I-dontknowbutlove."

The Influencer tries to take a sexy yet helpless selfie when Tom catches sight of her phone. He tosses the fishing line aside and charges straight toward her. Out of breath, he screams, "You've had a phone this whole time and didn't say anything?

I thought we were completely alone and that I'd be stuck here for the rest of my life with you!"

"Hello! It's my phone? Do you think I'd just hand over my phone to anyone? Jesus, not even my mom, dad, grandma, or my siblings got to touch my phone. What year do you think I'm from?" the Influencer snaps back. Tom tries to hold back, but he can't. He explodes: "Do you realize how stupid that sounds?! We're stranded on a deserted island, and the world could have ended. We don't know what's happening, and here you are with a phone?! A phone we could use to figure out where we are, or send out an SOS message so we can get the hell out of here?!"

"Jesus, chill, take a pill! It's just an iPhone. I had an iMac, MacBook Air, iPad, you name it! Galaxy was lined up to sponsor me, like, for real," the Influencer says proudly. "That makes no sense!" yells Tom.

"Ok, we need to use the phone and get in touch with someone," says Tom, as the Influencer starts tapping on her phone. "What are you doing?" The Influencer rolls her eyes, clearly annoyed by the interruption. "I'm talking to JulieTheSurvivor. We've really bonded over the past week."

"A WEEK? YOU'VE HAD A PHONE FOR A WEEK? Are you out of your mind? I've been walking around, pulling my hair out. I talked to a fish that I pulled out of the water, hoping it would understand me. For all we know, this is a post-apocalyptic world, and maybe it turned into a mutant fish, and maybe it could talk and pass the message on to someone who could rescue us and say, *'Hey, look at me. I'm a talking fish, and there's a Tom stuck on an island over there, and he needs to get off that place!'"*

"Lol, you talked to a fish? I've got to tell JulieTheSurvivor about this." Tom sneakily glances at her screen and sees that she has only 2% battery left. "You've only got 2% left? WHAT? That can't be possible! How much battery did it have when you found it?" asks Tom. The Influencer is wary, knowing that if she tells the truth, he'll go ballistic. "I promise I won't get mad," says Tom, as soothingly as he can. The Influencer smiles and says, "You pinkie swear?" Tom nods and smiles. "I had about 50% battery when I woke up. But then I found a power bank in my bag and was able to charge it a couple more times, thankfully! It's empty now, though... It really sucks. Julie and I had so much to talk about; she just gets what I'm going through."

"ARE YOU OUT OF YOUR MIND?!" yells Tom.
"You pinkie swore!"
"I've had enough! Give me the phone! I need to talk to someone who can get us out of here!" says Tom before starting to pull on the phone.
"Stop it, it's my phone!"
"Your phone, my phone, I don't care! Maybe it's the fish's phone that's actually a mutant!"
"YOU'RE CRAZY!"

Tom and the Influencer shove each other, fighting over the phone. Suddenly, it slips out of their hands and plunges into the water. "NO! Now I'll never get to talk to JulieTheSurvivor again! She was going to give me more tips on surviving on a deserted island!" the Influencer exclaims, starting to cry. Tom spots the fish he had previously suspected was mutated. The fish swims toward the phone, and... plop, it disappears into its belly. "That fish knew it was a phone!" shouts Tom loudly. He laughs hysterically before diving into the water and swimming after it, yelling, "FISH!" The Influencer remains indifferent. She bends down and unhooks the watchband from around her ankle, proudly looking at the brand-new Apple Watch she received as a Christmas gift from her ex.

"Hey Siri, call JulieTheSurvivor."

In a cramped and sweaty office, a group of anonymous people watch the drama unfolding on the deserted island. Unbeknownst to Tom and the Influencer, they're part of a reality show. Some take notes on what's happening on the screens, while others switch between different camera angles. Everything is staged. Everything is fake. We follow Tom's desperate attempt to swim after the fish, trailed by a yellow stream of urine in the water. "Now that's what I call multitasking," says one of the men as he nods approvingly at the screen. "Respect." The boss, wearing a tight and worn-out Ex on the Beach t-shirt, starts clapping. The rest of the room joins in, and it turns into a standing ovation. "This is real TV, folks! We're making history! Guri, add a more dramatic grade and see if we can CGI some menacing sharks in the background. Ali, have you got approval from Tix to use 'Doomsday'? We need some pow-pow psychedelic music here! Kevin, steer the fish back to land. Let's see if we can milk this couple a bit more." The boss's eyes fill with tears; this is his big chance.

Taco Friday

Mexican: "Your taco, amigo."

Ola Nordmann: "Can I get some cheese on my taco?"

Mexican: [shocked] "Are you American?"

Ola Nordmann: "No... Why do you think that?"

Mexican: "Because Americans love to destroy a good taco with a lot of cheese... But where are you from?"

Ola Nordmann: "Norway"

Mexican: [shaking head] "So the entire world loves to destroy a good taco with cheese... What's your name, gringo?"

Ola Nordmann: "Ola Nordmann!"

Mexican: "So tacos are very popular in Norway?"

Ola Nordmann: "Yes, very, very popular! We have something we call Taco Friday!" [takes a big bite of his authentic Mexican taco, with marinated beef, oregano, ground black pepper, cumin, paprika, lime juice, and chili, topped with fresh cilantro and finely chopped onion]

Mexican: [confused] "What do you mean Taco Friday?"
Ola Nordmann: "Taco Friday! We only eat tacos on Fridays, haha!"
Mexican: [laughs] "You're kidding me, right? ... Tacos are for every day, holmes."

Ola Nordmann: "But not in Norway, in Norway we eat tacos on Friday."
Mexican: "That's crazy, holmes. Why would you only eat tacos on Friday? What about Monday, Tuesday, Wednesday, Thursday, Saturday, and Sunday?"
Ola Nordmann: "Yeah... Good point, but in Norway, we only eat tacos on Friday."
Passing Mexican: "What's going on here, holmes?"
Mexican: "I'm talking to this gringo from Norway! He's telling me they only eat tacos on Friday, and it's called Taco Friday!"
Passing Mexican: "What's so special about Friday?"

Ola Nordmann: [looks confused at both] "In Norway... we have Taco Friday! On Tuesday we have fish, on Monday we have meat-free meals. Saturday is pizza. It's very simple!"

A few days later, on the national news channel in Mexico, everyone is following the interview with Ola Nordmann.

News Anchor: "Breaking news, Mexico. Lalito was selling

tacos just like any other day. But one day, this gringo from Norway came and bought a taco. Lalito, could you tell us what happened, in your own words, please?"

Lalito: "Hola Mexico, it was just a regular day, and I was selling tacos when this gringo came and bought some. So I asked him: You got tacos where you're from? He tells me: Yes, we got tacos, and we got something called Taco Friday. And I was like: What's that? He was like: We only eat tacos on Friday. And I was like: What's so special about Friday? He was like: Nothing. Crazy, right? Tacos are for every day... And I want to say hola to Bonita, my wife, and my kids Sanches and Poncho, and what's up to my cousin Miguel. Still bringing people from Mexico to the United States, holmes. Still making the family proud. Fuck Trump and his wall."

News Anchor: "Thank you, Lalito. This is a peculiar case. We will finally hear more about this bizarre phenomenon from Ola Nordmann himself... Ola, what is this Taco Friday all about?"

Ola Nordmann: [swallows nervously] "Well, in Norway, we have Taco Friday... That means that we only eat tacos on Friday."

News Anchor: "So strange... Why only on Friday? Is there anything special about Friday? And not Saturday, Sunday, Monday, Tuesday, Wednesday, or Thursday?"

Ola Nordmann: "I do not know why. It's just the way it is; Friday is for tacos."

Three men in dark suits march in and pull Ola Nordmann out of the studio.

News Anchor: "I was just informed that these men are from the National Security of Mexico, and that El Presidente is here."

El Presidente enters the room, and everything goes silent. He sits down next to the news anchor.

News Anchor: "What do you make of all this?"
El Presidente: "Señorita, this Taco Friday is an odd case; I haven't seen anything this bizarre since I watched the movie The Lobster. That's a very strange movie! We, the Mexican people, need some answers, so this is a message to Norway. We will keep Ola Nordmann here in Mexico until we get some answers about this Taco Friday. Why? I don't get it. And if you have some insight into the movie The Lobster, please send me that as well."

The news of Ola Nordmann's detention has reached Norway, and the media is searching for answers about what the authorities plan to do.

Reporter: "What does the government plan to do to bring Ola Nordmann back?"
Norwegian Foreign Minister: "I will travel to Mexico and

speak with El Presidente to get Ola back; this is just a big misunderstanding. We have always had a good relationship with Mexico."

Back in Mexico.

El Presidente: "I need you to explain this to me. What is this Taco Friday?"

Foreign Minister: "Well... just like Ola said, it's just Tacofriday, something that Norwegians love to do."

El Presidente: "Why?"

Norwegian Foreign Minister: "I do not know why..."

El Presidente: "Why not?"

Norwegian Foreign Minister: "I really do not know. I think this is just silly, and Ola Nordmann should be allowed to come back home!"

El Presidente: "Silly, you say? Did you find any insight about why people like the movie The Lobster?"

Norwegian Foreign Minister: "No... can Ola come home now?"

Back in Norway.

Norwegian Prime Minister: "The situation is such that the Foreign Minister and Ola Nordmann can't come home since none of us can explain why we have Tacofriday - why exactly on a Friday and why exactly taco. We've had a team working for weeks doing research, but we haven't reached a conclusion yet. Therefore, the government has decided that we will no longer have Tacofriday; now, it's just called taco. You eat taco, but don't call it Tacofriday. We sell tacos every day, and you can make tacos anytime, and there are taco deals every day, not just on Fridays. Now we have tacos every day, just like they do in Mexico."

Back in Mexico.

El Presidente: "We made Norwegians think we don't know about Taco Friday."
Danny Trejo: [laughs] "You crazy, El Presidente, I love Taco Friday, it's the best..."

What if we were honest in job interviews?

Boss: "Do you have any previous work experience?"

Drug Dealer: "Work experience? Sheesh... I've got so much work experience that peeps used to hit me up 24/7 'cause I was always on deck, ya dig? I started slangin' glue back in elementary school. No cap, them white kids went cray-cray for glue. Slingin' glue was smooth like peddlin' my sis's used undies, bro. Used panties? Solid biz. But forget that, that was small potatoes. In high school, Ali and I started pushin' hash, and it was easy breezy, no sweat. Ya feel me? I'd slice that slab up, sell it, and chop chop, puff puff, puff! Then we stepped up to coke, and we were like El Chapo Jr. But that stuff was hella risky, Narcos level. So, in the end, I thought; I gotta snag me a legit gig, clean up my act. Get a crib, a lady, and maybe a lil' Rottweiler. So yeah, you could say I've been hustlin' my whole life. Oh, and if you need a hookup, just holla at your boy."

Boss: "Why do you want to work for us?"

Gold Digger: "Oh my God, I am just insanely excited about working for you guys! Like, 180% totes for real! If you want to climb the social ladder, you gotta start somewhere, darling. Just think, in stores like this, that's where the crème de la crème come. Time to perk up the chest, plump those lips, and look a million dollars, because when you least expect it, Prince Charming will come riding on his white horse, or Porsche, you know. Luckily, I'm an extra small size because this lifestyle isn't for everyone. Money for food? Oh no, baby. Everything goes to designer clothes, a chic pied-à-terre, and teeth whitening. Thank God I get a discount when I start here! Time to stock up on posh hand soap and scented candles! Because if there's one thing daddy likes, it's a pristine little girl... You get me? After a couple of shifts here, I must have found myself a wealthier man than Cathrine. She snagged a slightly pudgy guy with beaucoup potential, though lots of back hair... but with money, everything can be fixed, am I right?? She's preggers now and lives in the 'burbs with last year's Tesla and a mother-in-law from hell. Thank God she got super fat, just imagine how saggy she's going to be after squeezing out that chubby baby! So yeah, my motivation has never been greater! You gotta put that rock on the finger, baby!"

Boss: "What do you hope to gain from this job?"

Thief: "Yo, to be straight up honest, my dude? I want your job. Nah, actually, I want the whole joint. So many dope things...

I'll never be late, and I'll be mad keen on workin' overtime. Need extra hands for Christmas, New Year's, or Easter? I'm your man! I wanna learn everything you know, soak up all the systems, budgets, preferably all the PIN codes, shift schedules, who and when peeps come to work, where the security cams are – I wanna know it all, ya feel me? In other words, you can trust me to get the job done, bro."

The Man Without Shame

On an early morning at a quiet café, I sit waiting for him – the man I'm going to interview, the man everyone's talking about. I catch a whiff of a delightful perfume. My nose follows the scent, leading me to the queue. There, I spot a well-dressed man in his thirties. With a voice that charms the lady behind the cash register. His appearance is a feast for the eyes.

He buys a coffee for himself and one for me. How he could tell my coffee cup was empty, I'm still a bit unsure about. But it's a nice move. With a firm grip on my hand, he introduces himself: "Bob." "Bob is an unusual name," I think, "Bob sounds like a hunter with a beer belly." With a flirtatious smile and a twinkle in my eye, I dive straight in: "How, or when, did you figure out that you should ask girls outright if they want to have sex with you?"

Bob replies nonchalantly: "Sex, what's wrong with that? Do you want to have sex with me? Should we have sex?"

I'm a little unsure if he's actually asking me, so I let him continue talking. "Norway has been ranked as one of the countries with the most one-night stands in the world. We love alcohol, we love parties. How many do you think love going out every weekend?"

I don't respond – there's something beautiful in what he's saying, and I'm curious about where he's going with this. "Very many" is the answer! I assume that every bar and club can accommodate over 100 people, and on a Saturday night in downtown Oslo, almost all the venues are packed. In other words, thousands of people go out on the town every weekend, and half of these are women. Most come to drink and dance with friends, others to mingle, and some to take a lucky one home. I, like many other men, go out to get laid."
He pauses, not to think it seems, but to make sure I'm following his words.

"What do you want me to do? Charm you senseless and make you like me? *Hey, what are you up to? What do you like? What do you want in life? Who are you? Who's your friend? Where have you been tonight?* I get tired just thinking about the answers I don't even care about. So you come home with me after I've bought you drinks and made you believe I'm the most wonderful man you've ever met. You think: I like him, maybe he's the one, he cares about what I say, he asks what I want, he asks what my friend wants!"

I still keep my mouth shut. This is just getting better and better.

"This is all just lies. Why can't we just look each other in the eye and say, without a filter: *Hey, do you want to sleep with me? Should we go home and have amazing sex?*
Without commitments, without pretending I want to be with you. What's wrong with that? If you feel offended, ask yourself why can't we say it? Why can't you say it? Don't you, like everyone else, have desires and needs that must be fulfilled every once in a while?"

"Many women believe that you make them seem like some kind of whore?" I say, challenging him, "I don't even know what that's supposed to mean, I don't pay anyone for sex. At best, we pay each other with a shared experience. I'm just a man who doesn't want to waste time pretending to care. I just want to have sex with you." He gets up to go to the bathroom, leaving me with a thousand questions. Is this a man who has cracked some code and found a new way to pick up women? Is this something everyone should do?

He returns with the same pleasant and tantalizing energy. "Do you think I'm being unreasonable, or do you feel I have a point in what I'm saying?"
"I'm not here to answer what's right or what's unreasonable; I'm here to interview you. You're a phenomenon everyone is

talking about. *You have to talk to Bob! Have you slept with Bob? Have you heard about how he picks up women?"*

Bob confidently settles back into his chair. "Just think about how accustomed we've become to people lying to each other, and we call each other 'players' or 'whores' because we get hurt. Imagine if everyone were honest about what they wanted instead of beating around the bush and pretending they want something else. I do what most people want to do, but don't dare. I choose to try, I don't succeed every time, but I do succeed..."

Bob stares at me, looks deeply into my eyes, and asks, "Do you want to have sex?"

We lie naked in bed, gazing into each other's eyes. "That was bloody amazing," he says, caressing my nipples. I rise and stand before the bed, his gaze still admiring my feminine curves. I grab the back of my head and pull off my disguise—my human suit elegantly falls away. Just like a human screams when they see a spider, Bob shrieks in terror. He shudders and trembles in fear. Humans handle this poorly, and Bob is no exception. He stares at me. He sees my large eyes without pupils, my grayish body devoid of human contours, the skin on the floor, and wonders where his penis has been.

I pick up a small frozen bubble from the skin, containing his semen. Bob tries to compose himself and stammers, "Wh... what is that?!"

"It's your semen, frozen," I reply.

Bob doesn't know what to say or do. His eyes dart around the room as quickly as his heart beats. His pulse is higher than I've ever recorded. I'm surprised his heart can handle this. "You're probably wondering what I am? I'm a being from another solar system. I came to this planet to have sex with you, Bob. We've studied you and concluded that you have a unique approach to getting laid. It's direct, honest, and effective. Had it not been for contraception, you'd be the father of hundreds of children. Now, I'm going back to my world to share this experience so we can learn from your wisdom and evolve sexually."

Bob tries to pull himself together, trembling as he attempts to speak: "S... so you're not a reporter, you're not a woman?"
"We have no genders where I come from. Did you really think a reporter would care about a man who goes around asking women if they want to have sex with him? As a final step in the evaluation, I had to hear the truth about why you do what you do, so I pretended to be a reporter. You passed with flying colors, Bob, and I want to thank you for your cooperation. The semen was thawing, and I have to leave quickly." A portal opens before us. "Goodbye, never see you again," I say and leave, relieved that Bob won't take it too personally.

It's been over ten years since I met Bob. The research I conducted saved our planet, and our population has grown like never before. We've advanced greatly in our sexual evolution, and we'll be forever grateful to Bob. That's why we've built a statue in honor of Bob, so we can always look up at his face and know that this is the man who saved us.

Unfortunately, humans don't see Bob the way we do. Bob is locked away in a psychiatric ward, staring blankly into space and waving his arms for a portal. Bob began grabbing women's vagina to check for a bubble underneath and then screamed, "DO YOU WANT TO HAVE SEX?" As a result, the staff at the psychiatric ward believe Bob's hands should be restrained around the clock. On my planet, Bob is remembered as "The Man Without Shame."

Honest Terrorist Recruitment

Hey, bro!

Bro, you easy be manipulate and believe all things you hear in mosque? Then you in right place, my friend.

You have no friends and believe everything from strangers? I talk to you.

You believe in God and not sure what do with life? You single and scared being forced marry your cousin? You not have job and try find meaning in life?

Then, my friend, God bring you right place.

We like brotherhood, real deal. No ladies in group, for real. We wear like them, just for hide, mix with niqab people. I swear, sometimes this trick work too good. I can't know who under niqab at home. My wife or brotherhood guy joking with me? I go off topic. Anyway, if you easy be fool, no job, nothing do, no girlfriend, and scared of cousin, then our brotherhood-terrorist group perfect for you.

Here, we all brothers, even in niqabs. Only thing you do is learn tell who is who by looking in eyes. Niqabs confusing, man. There courses for this, I tell you try! Strange we no start own course... We could make good money, really... We talk about that later!

Just one thing... Don't wear niqab pretend be my wife. I get little nervous about who I had sex with yesterday... Because my wife ask me in deep voice to take her behind... It real problem; I still think about it. Was that really my wife? So, from now, no niqabs in my house…

Back to recruit program, bro.

Wonder what happen after die? Me too, but I hope God no have ladies in niqabs there. 72 virgins good, but no need niqabs. That just confusing with 72 virgins in niqabs.
Join our brotherhood, we be brothers, always, in this life and next. Then you have chance to die in God's name and get 72 virgins, hopefully no niqabs, but we no promise.
So, my brother, don't think just do! By way, ticket here cost about 8–10,000 dollars... Sorry, should say that before, but let's not make about money!

Come to *****, meet us at ****, and brother in niqab will say hi. It just for hide; I hope that okay.

Join our brotherhood! We promise you never forget it!

Honest White Extremist Recruitment

Howdy there, white brother or white sister!

Y'all white and just love hatin' for no dang reason? Well, our white extremist group is just the ticket for ya.

You reckon all them foreigners wanna blow up our beautiful country? Perfect!

Now, we mostly got men 'round these parts, but we got some lady folk too. We ain't that messed up. We ain't like them Honest Terrorists; we need women. Somebody's gotta cook our food, right? Somebody's gotta sew our fancy uniforms; matchin' green jackets with them handmade silver cuffs. So darn stylish... I'm gettin' off track here. Y'all like marchin' in the streets in them snazzy green uniforms and hollerin' all sorts of nonsense? Well, come on and join us!

If y'all white but got that dark hair, we reckon you oughta dye it blonde. You'll be treated better if you're a blonde with them blue eyes. It's just the way it is. Christoffer's a blonde with blue eyes, and he gets some real special treatment. But we don't much like Christoffer 'cause there's a rumor he's one of them gays. Yep, we don't like gays neither. We call ourselves white extremists, but we're more like white-and-straight extremists.

So, if you're white, straight, and can't stand them brown folks, sign up!

Now, y'all can't be likin' that foreign food. Or, you can like it, but you ain't allowed to eat it. As your first step of bein' one of us, we'll stick a chip up your butt. It'll sniff out the tiniest whiff of chili, and you're stuck eatin' meatballs in brown sauce forever. I suggest you eat what you love before joinin'. Trust me, you'll miss it. I used to hate my burnin' ass after a good Indian meal, but now I reckon my bum misses it.

It helps if you're Christian and believe God's a white, old man who wants to wipe out all them brown Muslims. Muslims ain't that important to us; it's just somethin' we make up. Helps us look like angry, powerful, white men (and a few women).

I done lost my train of thought. I hope y'all ain't scared off by the chip! Some of us white brothers figured out how to trick them butt-chips, so now we go out and eat kebabs and all that Indian food. It's dang good. Bet white chefs could make it even better.

Join our white extremist group now! Even though we've found a way to fool that chip, we still like the idea of stickin' somethin' up your ass..

But anyhow, HEIL HITLER! Even though he was one of them Jews, but we don't talk about that. Sign up today!

Yumyalaman - The true crime murder

Yumyalaman had planned everything down to the smallest detail, and there was nothing he had overlooked. He was absolutely certain of it. Now he stood, gazing up at the balcony of his latest victim – the grand finale. The murder that would make him world-famous. For the past seven months, he had committed seven gruesome and incredibly clickbait-friendly murders. Each month, the police would find a new body, and each month, the police, newspapers, and famous conspiracy podcasters would hunt for the brutal but just Yumyalaman.

His journey to stardom began when he planned what to call himself. It had to be recognizable, something everyone would remember. Like a bolt from the blue, the name came to him: Yumyalaman. It was original and mysterious, maybe a bit hard to pronounce, but good enough. Everyone would fear his name, and no one would feel safe... For the man of justice would ensure that he was written into the history books and never, ever be forgotten.

For his first victim, he chose an elderly woman who had been out shopping, but she wasn't just any elderly woman. She was an elderly woman who bought unnecessary items. After killing her, he arranged a wreath of all the unnecessary items around her body and left a note that read: "She died because she bought unnecessary things, and you should think of this lady when you shop. Is this unnecessary? Do I really need this? Regards, Yumyalaman."

The first murder was perfect, but a bit sad, for the lady looked very sweet and had loads of delicious cakes in her kitchen cupboard. However, Yumyalaman believed he could make the world a better place. "Yumyalaman is not just a murderer; he also cares," he thought.

The second murder was an old, grumpy man. Yumyalaman left another note with the message: "All grumpy old men mustn't live. You're old, you're alive, be happy or cease to live. Otherwise, Yumyalaman will pay a visit. This is a warning to all the grumpy old men out there." Yumyalaman believed this would make old men stop being grumpy.

The third victim was a moose, and it was a carefully planned murder. This moose was one Yumyalaman had encountered many years ago, during a cabin trip with his classmates. One day, they suddenly crossed paths. They looked each other in the eyes and exchanged a few words. Yumyalaman went back and took the life of the moose. It was already dead and mounted on the wall in the dining room. But still, those lifeless glass eyes had provoked him. That very night, he left the stuffed head at the doorstep of the police station. In the third letter, it read: "This moose is the Moose of all moose, the Moose with a capital M. This Moose once said to me in my younger years: 'Come at me, bro.' After 22 years, I decided to take it literally, so I came after it and said, 'What's up? It's Yumyalaman!'"

The fourth and fifth murders were a couple living just outside Oslo. Yumyalaman thought they were disgusting pigs, and he wrote as much in the letter left for the police: "They're on welfare, complaining when they could actually work, and the worst part is that they're siblings. Yumyalaman doesn't like such pigs." Even though it turned out they weren't actually siblings, he was adamant that they were. It was just the media trying to manipulate the truth to cast Yumyalaman in a bad light.

The sixth and seventh murders were two roommates. This murder was meant to resemble an old Japanese film. In the letter, it read: "This is like an old Japanese film, except it's real. Yumyalaman." Yumyalaman decided not to explain why he killed the last two people. "If they're going to make a true crime series about this, they'll need something to investigate. That'll automatically add an extra episode," he thought. Yumyalaman delighted in all the conspiracy theories people around the world would speculate about; the internet was going to explode! This was going to be the most popular true crime series ever made.

It was now the eighth month, and he was ready to kill the final victim on his list. Yumyalaman stood, looking up at the victim's balcony. Every evening around nine o'clock, the man would come out to smoke. Yumyalaman recognized the stench, the stench of marijuana. "Only hipsters smoke marijuana," he thought, and he was going to put an end to that. Yumyalaman had planned this for a long time. When the Hipster finished smoking, he would ring the doorbell and ask to be let into the building. Yumyalaman figured the Hipster would let him in because he was clearly an idiot. The Hipster finished smoking and went inside. Yumyalaman rang the doorbell: "Hey, I forgot my key, can you...?"

Before he could finish speaking, the Hipster let him in. Yumyalaman chuckled to himself, thinking, "Idiot, haven't you learned? Never let strangers in... maybe they're a serial killer." Yumyalaman stood outside the Hipster's front door. This was to be his final murder, and it was to be the most gruesome and brutal murder ever. He had never been nervous before any of the other murders, but now tiny beads of stress sweat adorned his forehead. It was here he would be discovered and here he would take his own life before the police arrived. This was all carefully planned. He had to die for his grand and ingenious plan to be realized.

Suddenly, Yumyalaman kicked down the door. The Hipster

was in the process of eating a perfectly prepared hipster burger – meat from a local butcher, organic tomato and cucumber, topped with homemade chipotle sauce. With the burger halfway in his mouth, he looked in shock at the intruder.

"Look at me, don't look at the knives on the kitchen counter. Look at me, don't look at the hot food on the kitchen table. Look at me, I'm here to kill you, and there's nothing you can do to stop me. Just look at me," said Yumyalaman.

The Hipster smiled: "Why do you keep telling me to look at you?"

Why wasn't he afraid? Why wasn't he resisting? What was happening? "Because you've smoked marijuana, and it causes hallucinations, so I need you to focus on me," replied Yumyalaman.

"I guess you've never smoked marijuana before?" "No."

Yumyalaman pulled out a large knife from his pocket.

"Wow, is that the knife from the Rambo movie?" asked the Hipster.

"It is, and... NOW YOU'RE GOING TO DIE!" replied Yumyalaman.

"WAIT, WAIT, WAIT... hear me out. You're going to kill me, right?" "Yes?"

"Can I at least have a final meal? I've spent way too many years perfecting this sauce, and I think I've cracked the code. The trick is to let it steam with pine needles for 48 hours!"

Yumyalaman figured it was fair; considering what he planned to do to this poor guy, he could at least grant him a final meal.

"You may have a final meal," said Yumyalaman.

"Before we eat, would you like to have a little smoke with me? Please? It's my last day. My favorite thing is to smoke with others; you'd grant me that, right? Give me someone to smoke with, and you can do whatever you want with me. I won't stop you."

"Haha... What an idiot. Just for a few puffs, I can do whatever I want with him without any resistance. I can't pass that up," thought Yumyalaman. "Alright, I'll grant you that."

They stepped out onto the balcony. "So this is what it looks like from up here?" said Yumyalaman as he leaned over the railing. The Hipster lit the joint and took a hit before passing it to Yumyalaman. "So you've been keeping an eye on me?" asked the Hipster. Yumyalaman cautiously took a drag from the joint. "Hold your breath before you exhale," grinned the Hipster. Yumyalaman tried his best but had a violent coughing fit. "Damn, that stings... Yes, I've been watching you, noting when you smoke and how often. I've observed people's reactions as they walk by and also noticed who else in your neighborhood smokes," answered Yumyalaman.

"Fascinating. Are there many people in my neighborhood who smoke then?"

"Yes, it seems there are quite a few. But anyway, everyone who smokes that stuff is stupid."

"Why's that?" asked the Hipster.

"Because marijuana is a drug and it's illegal. It makes you dumb and leads to other drugs. Everyone who smokes marijuana is just a person without ambition," replied Yumyalaman.

"So you're saying that Golden Globe- and Emmy-winning Patrick Stewart is a guy without ambition? He said in 2017 that he smoked marijuana almost every day as an alternative pain treatment. Just like people drink alcohol, many also smoke when the occasion calls for it. Take Jennifer Aniston, for example. She said in a Rolling Stone interview that she likes to smoke once in a while. There's nothing wrong with that. I wouldn't call myself a stoner. Are both of these people dumb and without ambition?"

"But..." said Yumyalaman.

"Wait, I'm not done... Carl Sagan was an astronomer, cosmologist, astrophysicist, astrobiologist, author, and science communicator. Is he dumb too? Or Steve Jobs, do you really need me to tell you who he is? If you want to know how smart he was, just look at the iPhone in your pocket... Did you know alcohol is 114 times more dangerous than marijuana? Did you know no one has ever died from marijuana? Did you know someone tried to overdose on marijuana? Do you know what happened to him?"

"No," replied Yumyalaman.

"He just fell asleep. We have people dying from alcohol every day all over the world, but no one seems to care. Instead, we meet up the day after and laugh and chuckle about how foolish and drunk we were," continued the Hipster, passionately.

"Why is it illegal today, then? And why do people say it leads to other drugs?"

"That's a very long story, but I'll try to give you the short version. Hemp was the known term before marijuana. Harry Anslinger, the man responsible for stigmatizing marijuana and starting the DEA, once said that *marijuana is the most violence-causing drug in the history of mankind... Most marijuana smokers are Negroes, Hispanics, Filipinos, and entertainers. Their satanic music, jazz, and swing result from marijuana usage. Anslinger also said that reefer makes darkies think they're as good as white men – the primary reason to outlaw marijuana is its effect on degenerate races.* With such stories and politicians who had no clue about what was true or not, it was completely removed from society. In fact, research shows that marijuana can help with cancer, epilepsy, and has had a positive effect on people struggling with depression and anxiety," proudly stated the Hipster.

Yumyalaman found the Hipster's words fascinating, as this was information he had never heard before. "But why is it illegal in Norway?"

"Politics, my friend, politics. But that's another story," said the Hipster, signaling Yumyalaman to take another puff.

"I assume you don't have a job since you've had so much time to spy on me?" Yumyalaman laughed and took a couple more puffs from the joint, which was now finished.

"Come on, let's eat." "We?"

Yumyalaman reentered the apartment and saw the burger on the dining table. His mouth was parched, and his stomach was screaming for food. The Hipster opened the fridge. "Do you want a beer?" "Yes!" Yumyalaman took a big gulp of the beer; it was the best beer he had ever tasted. Before he could ask to taste a bit of the burger, the Hipster had already prepared one for him. "Thanks." Yumyalaman thought he had to stop fooling around; he couldn't thank someone he was about to kill. They sat down and devoured the food. The Hipster observed how Yumyalaman enjoyed the perfectly cooked burger: "What you're experiencing right now is the munchies."

"What's that?" asked Yumyalaman.

"Munchies are what you get when you smoke marijuana. You have THC in your body, and it makes your body think you're hungry, and it also gives you a really dry mouth."

Yumyalaman started laughing uncontrollably, "munchies..." In less than two minutes, they had eaten all the food. "What's your name? If I may ask."

"Yumyalaman."

"Yumyalaman, huh? The serial killer who has murdered seven, soon to be eight, people?"

Yumyalaman nodded and stared at the table, noticing a small scratch. "That killing will have to wait a bit. I'm so stuffed, and the beer made me dizzy."

"Just relax as long as you want. We have a deal, and I'll stick to it. Since you're going to kill me anyway, could you tell me why you killed all those people?" asked the Hipster.

Yumyalaman figured he was looking at a dead man – what could be so dangerous about telling him everything? And so, Yumyalaman started spilling every tiny detail to the Hipster. He felt so proud of what he had accomplished, and it was so great to finally share it with someone! "People will talk about this for years and will definitely make a true crime series about me! They'll never get answers to why I did this and what drove me to kill all these people. What was wrong with him? Why did he change his name to Yumyalaman? I'll be the ultimate true crime killer among all true crime killers. I'll go down in history books as the worst and smartest true crime murderer!" Yumyalaman was starting to come down from his marijuana high and could finally think more clearly. "Now it's time," he said, standing up. The Hipster began to laugh.

"What's so funny?" asked Yumyalaman angrily.
"Haha, you said you planned everything down to the smallest detail. You obviously haven't," said the Hipster.
"What do you mean?" Yumyalaman suddenly began to panic. Had the Hipster managed to alert the police? Were they already on their way to apprehend him?

"Haha, you can relax. I didn't call the police, but you clearly didn't plan on smoking a joint with me and eating my food. I know you've been stalking me for the past month; I've seen you from my balcony every single night, actually. Little tip: when you're sitting on a dimly lit balcony, you can see pretty clearly what's happening down on the street. Streetlights, my friend, streetlights."

Yumyalaman didn't like what he heard and pulled out his Rambo knife.

"Take it easy with that enormous Rambo knife of yours; now, listen, because this only gets better. To put it mildly, I got paranoid when you showed up every night staring at me with that intense look you've got right now... Maybe that's just how you look? Naturally resting, crazy bitch face? So, last week, I had my buddy dress up like me and sit on the balcony with a fat, juicy spliff. Meanwhile, I hid in the bushes behind you and watched up close what you were doing. When he finished and you moved on, I followed you. I trailed you to another apartment and saw through the window that you pulled out a sword and, like a true serial killer, slaughtered those living there. To be honest, it looked like a scene from a Japanese horror film. I read what you wrote about it being a Japanese horror film scene, only now it was real. That was a cool touch."

Yumyalaman started to smile; finally, someone understood him. Little by little, he loosened his grip on the massive Rambo knife. His ego loved this; he wanted to hear more. "You probably have many questions, and no, I won't contact the police. Now listen up..." The Hipster interrupted himself and went to the sink to get a glass of water.

"Yeah? Listen to what?"

The Hipster took a big gulp of cold water and fixed his gaze on Yumyalaman. "Yumyalaman. Haha... what a name... Yumyalaman. One thing you deserve applause for. I'd easily watch that true crime series. Random and brutal murders that don't make sense, imagine how many people are working to catch you right now. You're already the talk of the country!"

"Stop it, now I'm getting embarrassed," Yumyalaman had never had a friend before; was this what it felt like to have a real buddy?

"Since you've been so lax with your execution tonight, I'm guessing I'm your last victim, and today's the day you plan on getting caught. Big production companies will be lining up to make a true crime series about you!"

"Right?!"

"...but there's just one problem. I've filmed you; everything you've said in the last hour is on tape," said the Hipster, pointing to a camera in the ceiling. He pressed a pause button on his phone: "There, now everything's saved and sent to my cloud. You'll never get your hands on it now."

"WHAT?" yelled Yumyalaman.

"The whole world will know everything! So, the chances of a true crime series about you are minimal. You're just not exciting and mysterious anymore. But what they will make is a true crime series about the victim who caught the gruesome and stupid serial killer! How did he manage to film the killer without him knowing? Is he actually a super spy?"

"No... You wouldn't dare..."

"I'm going to be a star, the one who solved the mystery. Last week, I changed my name to Tingtrangling. Hahaha... Who'd want to be named Tingtrangling? It's a perfect name; no one else in the world has it! I'll be remembered forever! So, Yumyalaman, you can kill me now. I'm yours. Go ahead, fulfill my wish, or our wish, to become true crime celebrities," said the Hipster. He stretched out his arms and closed his eyes. With such a massive Rambo knife, it wouldn't take more than one swing to end it all. Yumyalaman paced around the dining table, screaming, "No, no, no! THIS IS MY TRUE CRIME SERIES!"

"Kill me, I'm ready, kill me now. So people can see my body on TV and talk about me, kill me."

"Are you stupid or what? No way I'm going to kill you now! Do you know how long I've been planning this? Do you know how much it sucks to be Yumyalaman? No one can even pronounce Yumyalaman properly! I thought I was a genius here, and then you come up with the name Tingtrangling, what the hell? It's even better than mine..."

Tingtrangling sighed, lowering his arms and approaching Yumyalaman. "What are you doing?" asked Yumyalaman.

"I'm trying to get killed, what do you think?"

"Let go of me, you maniac! I don't want to kill you!"

"Can you... keep your... arms... still!"

"I need to get out of here! Don't follow me; this is my true crime series!"

Yumyalaman dashed out the door and ran as fast as he could from the crazy Hipster. He had to get home and devise an emergency plan. First, he had to find and delete that video, then kill another random hipster, and finally himself, all ASAP. Tingtrangling let Yumyalaman go, for he obviously knew where Yumyalaman lived. He rubbed his hands together; the grand finale was just around the corner. Many hours later that same night, when Tingtrangling was sure Yumyalaman was sound asleep, he sent the video to the police. Then he entered Yumyalaman's apartment, found the Rambo knife, and lay down on the floor next to his bed.

Yumyalaman woke up early the next day, having slept poorly. If he couldn't fix this, he'd be just an ordinary loser who had watched too much Dirty John, and that was unacceptable. "A new day, new opportunities..." thought Yumyalaman as he turned to get out of bed. At that moment, he locked eyes with Tingtrangling. "Haha... my true crime series," said Tingtrangling, slashing his own throat with the Rambo knife. "NOOOOO!" Yumyalaman leaped out of bed and snatched the Rambo knife from Tingtrangling's hand. Suddenly, the door was kicked down, and a dozen police officers aimed their weapons at Yumyalaman.

"Yumyalaman, you're under arrest..." Yumyalaman looked in shock at his bloody hands and glanced at Tingtrangling. He was still alive... He was still alive, smirking wickedly at Yumyalaman: "My true cri..."
"NOOOO!!!"

Shoot First, Ask Later: A Diary.

Day 8,556

Dear Diary, you're the only one who understands me, who knows the code I live by—the code that has kept me alive all these years. Even though I have you, loneliness is starting to wear me down. I don't know what to do about it; I can't trust ANYONE. That's just how the world has become, and I've accepted it, but still. Just a hug, a smile, anything! But... that hug could end in a deadly head-lock, and that smile could be filled with acid, killing me in an instant. No, I must be grateful to have you, Diary.

Day 8,557

Even though I have no idea what day it is today, it really feels like a blue Monday. You get me, Diary; you understand what I mean. Today, I ventured out from my safe and secret bunker, the location of which even you don't know. I can't risk you betraying me and revealing its whereabouts. That's why I only write in you when I've turned off the lights, so you can't see your surroundings.

I hope you understand, Diary. I do it for your own good. I love you.

Day 8,558

Diary, I must tell you something important. You know me, you know how I am, you know what I've seen. I've seen people pull a knife out of a bowling ball... Knives from every conceivable hole. It's kill or be killed. Never again will it be: "Hey, shall we share what we have? Shall we be friends? Shall we try to rebuild society and live as civilized humans?" Never. Now I'm sad. We'll talk tomorrow, Diary.

Day 8,559

I haven't been entirely honest with you, Diary. Something happened on my trip on day 8,557. Don't get too excited now, but you'll get to come out of the dark closet and take a look at something. But before that, I must tell you what happened on that dreadful, dreadful journey.

You know better than me that I never go out during the day. I don't know why I did it, maybe an external force influenced me? Anyway, I went out, and as soon as I stepped out of my hidden bunker, I saw a woman... She looked at me... And you know how I live, I just react, but in that split second before I acted, I thought of all the things that could go wrong.

My first thought was that maybe she wasn't alone, that she was bait. I didn't want to go for that scenario; only amateurs do that. I'm no amateur.

My second thought was that she was going to make me fall in love with her. I haven't been with a woman in... You know what? I can't even remember the last time I was with someone, so there's a good chance I would've fallen head over heels. Then her plan would probably be to take over my bunker and kill me the day we ran out of food. Cut me up into little pieces, freeze me, and eat me in her Friday tacos.

The third thing I thought of was that maybe she was an extraterrestrial being who had taken human form. What could happen then? EVERYTHING. She could've kidnapped me and investigated how I had lived... She could've taken out my brain to see why I was so smart - a smart person with a smart philosophy: "Shoot first, ask later."

BOOM! I shot her right in the head, a freaking headshot. I breathed a sigh of relief, thinking it was a wise decision. When her body fell and it went quiet, I suddenly heard a baby crying. Do you hear, Diary? There was a baby. I walked over, and there lay a real human baby. I got scared. Because a crying baby attracts attention. A crying baby is food that hasn't been eaten yet. So, I had to bring the baby into the bunker. OH MY GOD, I have a baby in my bunker, I don't know how to take care of a baby. I think of everything that could go wrong with a baby! Oh no, it's crying now. What do I do? You know what, we'll have to deal with this tomorrow. Hang in there for one more day, my dear Diary.

Day 8,560

I'm back. That thing is just impossible, constantly eating, pooping, and sleeping at random! I haven't slept at all tonight... Diary, you know me, I just acted on instinct and brought the baby with me. Let me tell you about all the smart things I thought of before I picked it up from its mother's bloody arms. The first thing I thought was, what if I raise this little guy in this terrible post-apocalyptic world, and one day I die, then the child will grow up and become incredibly smart. And as the smartest one out here in the wasteland, he starts an army, because I've told him that no one has thought of starting an army and taking over vast territories. The boy's army grows, and he becomes hungry for more and more power. The kid becomes incredibly dangerous, and before anyone knows it, he's become the wasteland's most powerful ruler.

The second thing I thought was, what if it's actually a little alien baby? What if this woman was actually an alien lady who had given birth to an alien baby and made it look like a human baby? What if this baby is making crazy alien plans, plans that I will never understand? Then one day when I'm sleeping, this little guy comes and lays eggs in my stomach, and before I know it, fully grown aliens are digging their way out of my belly with their long, gross nails and killing me?

The third thing I thought was, what if this isn't a real baby and

I'm just imagining the whole thing? Have I eaten too many mushrooms? Am I that desperate for some contact? I need to relieve some pressure so I can see a little clearer what's real and what's not. Don't judge me now, Diary. You know the mountain goat and I have a professional relationship, friends with benefits. It's only you I love, don't forget that! Bye, kisses.

Day 8,561
My dear, beautiful, kind Diary! I feel 1000 kg lighter! I'm so happy! Don't be jealous now, we've tried, but your hard and dry paper pages just don't do the job for me. I still love you, you'll always be my number 1!

After a long and sweaty night, I see everything clearly now. I will keep the baby, and yes, it's real. But you know me, I've been thinking, how will this work? I think the child should learn to live by my code: shoot first, ask later. Over time, I'll probably grow incredibly fond of the child, but eventually, this child will become a teenager. What if this teenager develops feelings that I'm not aware of and gets into trouble, forcing me to leave my safe, little bunker to save him? What do I do then? What if during this journey, I almost die and tell him how his mother died? Then he'll be mad at me because his whole life has been a lie. And it's true, I didn't shoot him! I didn't shoot first and ask later! Ah, I'm so disappointed in myself. Can I live by this code, can I teach it, when I don't follow it myself?

Fortunately, this is just a baby, and I will raise this child by my rules. The rule is always the same, shoot first, ask later. For this to work, I must watch with hawk eyes to make sure he doesn't fall in love when he becomes a teenager, and I must make sure he never sees you. He must never know that I killed his mother and especially not that I didn't kill him!

You can come out and see him. But my dear Diary... You must die, you know too much. We've had such a great time together, but that time is over. Now it's me, the kid, and the mountain goat I tied to a tree further up the hill. Before you die, you can see the baby, and after that, I'll throw you onto the fire.

There, you saw the baby, that was it, it wasn't anything special, it looks like all other babies. I wasn't too surprised either. Goodbye, looking forward to the day we meet again. See you, Diary, you'll always be in my thoughts.

The Story They Don't Want Us to Know!

On a privately-owned island, one hundred and ten miles away from the mainland, the world's most powerful men had gathered. The island covered seven hundred hectares, had three mansions of eight thousand square meters each, and was owned by the three richest men in the world: Rich, Sultan, and Business. They demanded only the best of the best, so the island was teeming with the world's finest chefs cooking food from organic farms, the most attractive and skilled housekeepers from Thailand, and the toughest, most intimidating security guards from a country no one can pronounce. The airspace above the island had been purchased and erased from the world map. Protected by a secret military defense with no name or affiliation to any nation, they were ready for The Annual Meeting.

Rich, Sultan, and Business had summoned the 100 richest

and most powerful men from around the world to discuss potential new threats. With a clean-shaven chest and tight, tiny swim trunks, Rich took the microphone. In his other hand, he held a pink umbrella drink with "yolo" written on the umbrella. He looked out at the audience, who wouldn't stop talking. Rich grew angry and yelled into the microphone: "SILENCE." Everyone turned irritably toward Rich. How dare he dictate what they should do? Although Rich was the richest and most powerful man in the world, he was hardly much wealthier than the remaining 100. No, he needed to take a chill pill and significantly lower his expectations if they were going to get anything out of The Annual Meeting. The Sultan began to laugh because he was the second richest person in the world and, therefore, the second most important person in the room. The Sultan was the Sultan of all sultans. He had even patented the name Sultan, so no one else in the world could call themselves that. He had so much oil and gold that you might think he had patented those too. Completely drunk, he staggered toward the stage, and no one dared to stop him.

"Look at me!" Rich slammed the table. "I'm richer than all of you!" It still wasn't completely quiet. "Shut up, or I'll have Sultan chop off your heads!" Sultan crawled up onto the stage and was served a new beer by one of his seven wives. "YES! Shut up. I'll chop off your heads if you don't do as I say!" Rich took the floor again: "Now that I have your attention, we have a crisis in the world right now. Ordinary people are starting to get rich, and that's a problem. I can't allow other people to become as wealthy as me. Then we have no balance. Then I'm not special anymore."

Sultan belched into the microphone. "Oops, I'm not going to apologize for that... But we have a solution! We need to keep people dumb, for dumb people don't get rich." Sultan was interrupted by a guest who sprang up from his chair. Sultan screamed: "HIM," while pointing at the poor man who had unwittingly sat on a wasp. The Sultan's third wife ripped off her niqab, revealing her muscular body. Arnold Schwarzenegger would have stood no chance against this lady; she was the green Arabian Hulk. With a 17th-century saber made of Damascus steel, she sprinted toward the man and chopped off his head as if it were made of butter. "See? I'm not kidding. I own oil and gold. So, I can do whatever I want," said Sultan. "Okay... Awkward." Rich took a sip of his refreshing pink drink. "Back to what's important. We have decided to underpay all teachers in public schools. We must pay them so poorly that they can't make ends meet. And when you don't have enough money to support yourself or anyone else, well, then you become bitter and grumpy. Surrounded by bitter and grumpy teachers, the students will slowly but surely start to hate their lives too. This is the perfect vicious circle: Teachers won't bother teaching, and students will refuse to learn anything."

"Did you hear that? This is brilliant," said Sultan before bursting into another fit of laughter. Rich followed with a wicked grin, and soon the entire assembly was cheering wildly – the idea that ordinary people would never experience the good sides of life, where money wasn't a concern, made them ecstatic.

Rich: "We'll also give the smart students sedative pills and say they have some sort of diagnosis. With dull students, I think there's a golden opportunity to push some drugs on them at the same time. I'm rich, and I can buy all the narcotics in the world. We'll spread this around all the schools. What will they do? Stop us? It's us who started the war on drugs."

Out of the blue, a man in a suit walked up on stage and stood in front of Rich and Sultan. Rich saw that Sultan didn't like it, but before he could raise his arm, Rich stopped him and said, "It's okay; it's just Business. We need him right now, and maybe later too." Fortunately, Business didn't catch that. He was the man responsible for all business in the world, owning Silicon Valley and the World Bank. If you had a loan, a MasterCard, or a TV on installment, this was the man you owed money to.

Business: "Too many private businesses are being started today; we can't have that. So, I have a plan: Corona..." A fourth person rushed onto the stage, shouting, "I vote for world peace!"

Sultan screamed loudly, "Him!" and the Arabian female Hulk sprinted toward him, chopping off his head as well. Sultan kicked the head into the audience, blood spraying the guests. "I wish for world peace," he said ironically. Everyone burst into another fit of laughter. World peace was impossible; they had made sure of that. They laughed and laughed until they were interrupted by a large plane landing by the water. Out came Jeffrey Epstein and his guests. Everyone on the island ran towards the plane like a group of six-year-olds who had spotted an ice cream truck.

"I love our Annual Meeting," said Rich to Sultan and Business as he took a sip of his yolo-drink. They shamelessly watched the various ice pops dancing carefree on the beach. "Refreshing...," said Sultan. "Remember, I choose first; after all, I am the richest!" shouted Rich, pushing away the excited boys.

Back When Picking Up Girls Was *"Normal"*

Grandpa, at 98 years old, was the last true gentleman of his generation. But with age came bitterness. He couldn't die before expressing what had weighed on his heart for so long. With a paper background and cursive font, he wrote a final letter to his children and grandchildren on his old and frail iPad, hoping that these wise and insightful words could help them avoid the same disastrous fate.

My dears, December 3, 2092

I've just learned that I only have a few days left. Testicular cancer is not recommended. When the doctor explained why testicular cancer would be my downfall, I couldn't help but give a big "fuck-you" finger to the Bowerbird Man. I haven't had sex for sixty years because of this idiot. And no sex means no stimulation of the balls. The semen has become so old that it has turned to stone. Stone weighs a damn lot. Now my balls dangle between my legs, and when I put on my clothes, I have to shove them down one pant leg and into my sock. P.S.! Long socks are important! I don't want you following in my footsteps. Have sex, for crying out loud! Don't let your balls turn to stone! I want you to read this letter aloud to each other, and when the time is right, to your children and grandchildren.

Once upon a time, it was common to pick up girls at bars. Men usually started by saying, "Hi," and if the woman liked what she saw, she'd reply, "Hi" back. This led to small talk, perhaps about the latest Snapchat filter, and then they went home together and had sex. If the sex was good, they might exchange contact information and begin six months of texting and occasional hookups. It was important not to be too forward; the social code dictated that they shouldn't respond to a snap for at least two hours. Responding sooner made them seem clingy and led to ghosting. It was the Golden Age, and everyone was hooking up like horny monkeys – sexually transmitted infections were rampant! But then this idiot came along. A guy who was clearly still a virgin and ruined it for men worldwide. If I had known how much he would ruin for me, I would've taken him out on the spot.

This idiot couldn't pick up women the usual way and decided to mimic a certain bird. The bowerbird... God... I feel nauseous just writing the word. If you're not familiar with this bird, look it up. It says that male bowerbirds build elaborate structures to impress female bowerbirds. If the female bird likes what she sees, things end well. In other words, no stone balls for that bird.

He decided to build a house for the girl he liked. Right in front of her apartment, he began constructing a small, soon-to-be extravagant treehouse structure. Nobody understood what he was doing. "Oh, what are you up to?" "I'm building a house for the girl I'm in love with," he replied to everyone who asked. This stunt quickly gained notoriety, and soon the whole world was eagerly watching. Do you know what happened then? Women all around the world thought, "Oh my God! My man has never built a house for me!" No kidding? Do you know why your man has never built a house for you? Because just like you, he's working every day so that you can afford to live in the house you already have. You already have a house! Be grateful for what you have.

Here comes the plot twist: The girl he was in love with didn't even know who he was! Like a true stalker, this idiot had followed her and found out where she lived. Not only that, but he had also begun constructing a house outside her private residence. Why does no one think that's a bit strange? No, why does no one find that incredibly creepy? The big question that no one wondered about when this happened was how did he get permission to build a house in the middle of a public area without any approvals? A house right in the bustling heart of Oslo, where people struggle to buy a one-room apartment for over 3 000 000 dollars? And he's being hailed as romantic?

Get a grip, folks...

If this person had been darker-skinned, he would have been stopped right away. The girl would have called the police and said there was a stalker following her. Without any questions or room to explain his grand romantic gesture, the police would have taken him away, and she would never have seen him again. Afterwards, the whole neighborhood would say, "Good Lord! Here come these foreigners, building houses wherever they want." What also irritates me is this clueless girl. If she had just kept a low profile and not made such a big fuss, we could have avoided the rest of the female population comparing themselves and their future relationships to these two knuckleheads. NRK and other major international TV channels had set up cameras, and one could follow the construction process minute by minute. It was no secret that the house was being built for her, but when she was interviewed, she pretended to be surprised and said, "Is he building a dream house for me?" How blind can you be? If someone had built a house for me, I would have been grateful for whatever they managed to create. But no... When the girl realized she was getting a townhouse for free, she started milking it for all it was worth. On live TV, she began criticizing and demanding more and more from him. "No, there's a little hallway missing here, I want a walk-in closet, the bathroom doesn't have tiles..."

What's wrong with you? He's out here building a house for you, he's put his life on hold to do this for you! When the house was finished, the girl went on TV and said, "We have to celebrate with a vacation. Will you take me to the Canary Islands?" But what about the damn house he built for you? Aren't you going to live there for a few days before demanding even more from the poor fool? The whole world melted at this, it melted like a fresh soft-serve ice cream on a hot summer day. On live TV, they set the standard for all future and existing relationships. Now, no women would even talk to men unless they had a house. And even if they got a brand new house, it wasn't guaranteed that she would want him. Soon, women all over the world owned all the new constructions, and men were physically, mentally, and financially bankrupt.

Desperate men with blue balls so big that their pants no longer fit stood in all kinds of weather, building houses. No one was getting laid! On Saturday nights, I often saw men trying to build houses out of kebab leftovers. They looked pathetic. Others tried to be creative and made houses out of cardboard boxes. Cardboard boxes? What happens if I kick one of those? Are you moving? That was actually a common joke at the time. Fortunately, I found my dear Karianne long before this hysteria started. I felt lucky to have gotten off "cheaply," or so I thought. It didn't take long before she gave me an ultimatum. Despite being married for ten years and having three beautiful children, I had to declare my love for her, and it had to be shown through a brand new house. Even though I was a partner in a law firm and made a lot of money, that wasn't good enough. The big house in Bygdøy wasn't enough anymore. All the other wives in the area had gotten a mini-house in the garden, and

Karianne couldn't be the only one without a house, and the house had to look at least as nice as the others.

Karianne left me the following year. A young, newly trained builder with sexy manly hair all over his body had set up a three-story house next to my pathetic dollhouse in the garden. So incredibly rude. It didn't help that their bedroom window faced mine. There I was, lying in bed every night, watching him take her hard in doggy-style. Just the way she liked doggy-style...

My children, my grandchildren. Learn from me! Take my money and hit the town! Pick up ladies! If you forget me and my story, I've included a picture of my balls. Let it burn into your memories.

———————————

Chapter 3

Brain-Damage

MEETING WITH GOD

Believer: "God, I've been waiting for this moment my whole life."

God: "Why have you?"

Believer: "You are Omega, the Almighty, and the creator of everything."

God: "Well, yeah... but that's not so important. Tell me, what did you do with your life?"

Believer: "God, I devoted my entire life to you. I lived in the Vatican since I was young and prayed to you every day. I died as an old woman with nothing but my love for you. I am so grateful."

God: "What the hell?! So you stayed in one place your whole life? You never saw the world?"

Believer: "No..."

God: "Why did you do that?"

Believer: "Because it's a noble thing to do. I wanted to serve you. I didn't want to be a sinner; I wanted to serve you and do something good."

God: "I am God, Omega the Almighty as you say. I don't need anyone to serve me. Why would you give your life to me? I was the one who gave life to you."

Believer: "..."

What happened after Jesus was crucified.

Two influential and important men discuss what they should do after Jesus' death.

Important Man 1: "What's the deal with that Jesus guy who went around claiming to be God's son?"

Important Man 2 nods approvingly: "You can't just go around saying you're the boss's son; that's totally nuts."

Important Man 1: "What should we do about it, then?"

Important Man 2: "We should accomplish what he couldn't do himself."

Important Man 1: "What do you mean?"

Important Man 2: "Turn Jesus and God into an all-consuming, world-dominating religion. Spread his wisdom and message, and maybe make a buck or two in the process."

Important Man 1: "I see where you're going with this."
Important Man 2: "We'll make him a Messiah. It's a win-win for us! No one else has thought of claiming to be the son of the boss who supposedly created all this. We must milk this for all it's worth."

Important Man 1: "Absolutely! But how do we make that happen?"

Important Man 2: "We say he's God's son and that he died for our sins. It'll make people feel guilty, and they'll panic. WHAT? He died for us? Think about all those who threw stones at him as he carried that heavy cross."

Important Man 1: "Yeah... that's smart! I hit him right in the nuts. Poor guy, knocked the wind right out of him. I feel a bit guilty about that."

Important Man 2: "They'll believe they won't get into heaven. Then we can say they can be pardoned. But only if they can pay for their sins."

Important Man 1: "And we'll say that God's house should never be taxed! Because, why should God pay taxes?"

Important Man 2: "WE'RE GOING TO BE RICH."

Important Man 1: "But how do we know there won't be another Jesus? It could ruin everything."

Important Man 2: "We're the ones dictating history now; what we say is the truth. We can say Jesus will come back one day, but only we know who the real Jesus is. So if he comes back, we can just call him an imposter. I can't handle any more commotion. No, he shall remain a symbol and nothing more."

Important Man 1: "But how will we ensure that people do and continue as we say? We need some kind of leverage..."

Both stare at each other in silence.

Important Man 2: "I know how! We'll make ourselves even more important people, intermediaries to God, and say it's not enough to just buy their way out of sins. To become completely sin-free, they must also confide in us. If they don't, they'll end up in a place where they'll burn forever and ever."

Important Man 1: "Intriguing, think of all we can learn! But we need to package it nicely, and say we have a vow of silence or something."
Important Man 2: "Haha... Vow of silence..."

Important Man 1: "Imagine all the secrets we'll learn, from ordinary people to even-more-important-than-us people! Finally, we can get some insight into all the juicy gossip the ladies are holding onto!"

Important Man 2: "I love what I'm hearing."

Important Man 1: "But one thing, I've always wondered about this. If Jesus is God's son, and God isn't human, how was he born?"

Important Man 2: "I've thought about that too. Jesus could've at least patched up all the logical gaps before he died. Hmm... We'll just say his mother got pregnant out of the blue, but she's still a virgin. We need to include a holy and virginal woman who sets the standard for the rest of womankind. We can't keep stoning sexually liberated women every Friday forever."

Important Man 1: "Friday stoning is my favorite thing, though..."

Important Man 2: "We can't do that anymore, suddenly there will be no women left."

Important Man 1: "Ah, fine! But should we include a picture of God?"

Important Man 2: "Of course we should! Why not create paintings and statues? Picture this... We hang Jesus on the cross he died on, with lots of blood and gore... He looks down and is sad because he had to die for our sins. It's the first thing people see when they enter God's house. It's going to haunt them throughout their visit, and they'll do everything they can to make amends."

Important Man 1: "Haha... I love life! And we'll get that John who lives in the cave to write about the Apocalypse. He eats mushrooms all day and talks about the end of the world every chance he gets. He's perfect for the job."

Important Man 2: "I love myself, I love you, we're geniuses! I just hope those Arabs over the mountain don't steal our idea..." Important Man 1: "I totally forgot, there's a woman being stoned today. Should we join in and throw a stone or two? Just one last time?"

Important Man 2: "What did she do?"

Important Man 1: "They say she's a witch."

Important Man 2: "What exactly is a witch?"

Important Man 1: "Nobody knows. Come on, I know a guy who can give us a good deal on some really nice stones!"

Fake vs Real Muslim

Honest Father: "I'm going to be honest with you. My father wasn't honest with me, and it caused a lot of problems. It's not easy growing up as a Muslim, especially in a country with such diverse attitudes and values as Norway. But I've learned, and now I'll tell you who you can be and how it should be done. Let's start with Ali.

Ali, you can be what we call a Fake Muslim today. That means that when you get older, you can lie about praying, even though we know you never pray. You can pretend you're fasting during Ramadan. You can have sex with girls and pretend you're still a virgin. You can go out on the town, drink, and eat everything that isn't halal, because if you drink alcohol, you might as well eat pork too. What's the difference? People might see you, but they'll overlook it. After all, you're a boy.

But Fatima, you must be a Real Muslim; you can't do what Ali does. You can't drink, you can't sleep with boys, you can't eat anything other than halal meat. You're not a Fake Muslim.

But since I'm an honest father, I'll give you a tip. If you're going to be a Fake Muslim, you have to be a Ninja. I'll show you some tricks later, but you really need to fool the system. You can never let another Muslim man or woman see you out late at night; you must never be seen with a bottle of beer. Nobody should see you eating anything other than halal. That's the Ninja way. If any Muslims come and complain to me, I'll have to pretend to agree and feel ashamed for the family. That's just how the culture is. What did I say?"

Ali: "Fake Muslim!"

Fatima: "Ninja!"

Honest Father: "DONE!"

Where are my 72 Virgins?

Human: "God, I died in your name, and people told me I'd be rewarded with 72 virgins."

God: "Yeah, yeah... You'll get them, here they come."

Human: "What the hell? They look awful. This one doesn't even have legs, but you had time to make a wheelchair? What am I supposed to do with her? Push her around for all eternity? And what's this, an alien? Where's the hole, huh? And this is just ridiculous. Half donkey, half human? I don't even dare to look at the others!"

God: "DON'T MAKE ME ANGRY NOW. Do you know how many people want 72 virgins?! Look behind you!"
The human looks back, and the queue stretches as far as the eye can see.

God: "All those idiots behind you want 72 virgins. Do you know how long it takes to create 72 virgins?! A DAMN LONG TIME, I TELL YOU."

Angel: "God?"
God: "What do you want?"

Angel: "First of all, the virgin machine is broken, and these humans standing before you have actually killed innocent people they consider sinners and non-Muslims. They have died for you under the illusion that if they take their own lives as martyrs and take others with them in death, you will reward them with 72 virgins."

God: "What the hell... HEY, EVERYONE! You're all a bunch of idiots; you won't get a thing! Do you think I'm going to reward you with 72 virgins after you've killed innocent people? Nobody gets anything."

All the idiots nervously swallow – oops.

Human: "No, no, no! I'm very happy! I can totally have sex with an alien and I have no problem with the one in the wheelchair; I'll gladly push her around for all eternity! Super eco-friendly!"

The day Amir got slapped by the Imam.

A young 14-year-old Amir decides to ask the Imam some questions.

The day had come, and Amir and his buddies had gathered outside the mosque. They had all written down their questions in their notebooks, and Amir was ready to take one for the team – after all, he had the most absences from the mosque and was already labeled as a not-so-good Muslim. Amir was determined and thought that if this were to be his last Quran school lesson, why not go all in. The class had begun, and everyone sat with their heads bowed down in the Quran, listening to the reading. Amir raised his hand and interrupted the Imam.

"Amir?" said the Imam.
"Well, I was wondering... In our last class, you said that God

loves curious children, and the Quran tells us we must ask critical questions," said a nervous Amir.

The Imam smiled and replied, "My son, of course, you can ask critical questions. Do you want to ask me privately, or in front of the whole class, so we can all hear and discuss this together?"

"We can do it with the rest of the class," Amir responds.
Iman said, "Then we'll do it after we finish reading."

When the Quran session ends, everyone puts away their Quran and sits in front of the imam. Amir is nervous but tries not to show it to his classmates.
Imam: "So, what are you wondering, Amir?"

Amir takes a deep breath and looks at his notebook: "Everyone tells me that Norwegians are kafirs, that they aren't Muslims. I have a good friend named Henrik. Henrik is a kind kafir. You know what he did once? A boy at school called me a "fucking Muslim and a Paki". Henrik pushed him away and stood up for me. Henrik isn't a Muslim, but he does many good things, as if he's a good Muslim! I've thought a lot about this. It's not Henrik's fault that he isn't a Muslim, right? So whose fault is it, really? Is it his mother's fault? She's also very nice and always brings us chips and pizza when we're gaming. So it can't be her fault. Maybe it's her mother's fault? Now I'm confused; this is difficult. Whose fault is it that Henrik isn't a Muslim?"

The imam listens seriously. Before he can answer, Amir continues with his many existential thoughts and questions.

"I've thought a lot about this, and I'm sure many others here have friends who aren't Muslims but are good people. It's not their fault that they weren't born as Muslims. So if Henrik dies, will he not enter Paradise? I want to be friends with Henrik forever; he's my best friend. Is it fair that God chooses who is born Muslim and who isn't? Then He decides who goes to heaven and who doesn't. It seems like cheating, at least to me." The imam looks kindly at Amir. "All those who are not Muslim will enter paradise if they have had a pure heart and faith in God. They will also be welcome in God's house. Our Prophet, peace be upon him, will pray for those in Jahannam (hell), and everyone will have a place in God's house."

"Ok, that's good for Henrik. I'll tell him tomorrow. You know, it's not easy with all these heaven rules. Christian heaven, Jewish heaven, Muslim heaven, I heard Indians don't even have a heaven. They're born again and again, that must be exhausting." The imam smiled and laughed at Amir's curiosity.

Seeing that the imam wasn't angry, Amir continued, only now with a little more confidence and a little less filter: "Ok, next question! It's about Ahmed at school; he's a wild Muslim. Ahmed is in the tenth grade, and he's already had sex with a girl, or as he says, many girls." Amir paused and looked at the imam after saying sex. "Is it okay for me to talk about sex, because it's a pretty important question?"

The imam gestured for him to continue.

"Well, I've heard from adults that you shouldn't have sex before marriage and that you shouldn't watch porn. But you know, the other boys in my class watch porn and talk about sex all the time. It's like sex, gaming, sex, gaming, girls, sex, and gaming. I don't know how to handle it. It's hard being a Muslim today, you see... Let's address the sex question first... So a person shouldn't have sex before marriage, I know that. But can they watch porn? I don't know if I believe a person can hold out until they get married. Because Trond in my class, he, um, masturbates like eight times a day, and we're only in the 8th grade. The rest of us have bets on whether his penis will fall off." Amir became nervous; he had just said 'porn,' 'sex,' and 'masturbate' in the mosque. But he was determined; his questions were too important to back down now.

"Ok, so how should a young guy like me and everyone else here deal with sex, masturbation, and girls? Because we live in Norway, with entirely different values and attitudes and... temptations? I don't have any temptations right now, but I'm afraid that when I get older and these other girls get older, I'll become like Ahmed in the tenth grade. Trust me when I say this, Ahmed in the tenth, he's crazy."

The imam tried not to get angry with Amir in front of the class, when he asked these questions - he was just a young and curious boy. "Sexual intercourse is meant to be between a man and his wife. One should not have an open... um...

relationship with a person they are not married to. It is sinful to masturbate. A person only makes a fool of themselves when they rub their genitals for pleasure. As for pornography, it's a big NO, Muslims don't do that."

Amir became confused; he had never heard the word 'pornography.' "So God is against porno...graphy?"

"Yes, proper Muslims don't watch such nonsense. Instead, they pray and spend time with God."

"You have no idea how much porno...graphy is out there. Ahmed says that in the future, you'll only need to think about a naked woman, and porno...graphy will appear on your computer. If God knows about the internet and knows how much porno...graphy is out there, but forbids us to watch it, he must be trying to control it... That's what I think, anyway." Amir saw that the imam didn't like what he was saying. But he also had a responsibility to himself and the others to actually get answers to these important questions.

"When did you come to Norway?"
"I came to Norway when I was 18 years old, and today I am 44 years old."

The imam took a sip of his water; Amir let him drink before continuing. "So you've lived here for quite some time. During all these years, you must have seen a porn magazine, right?

Walked into a 7-Eleven and wondered what those magazines on the top shelf are?"

The imam spat out his water before shouting, "AMIR!"

"I'm just asking, don't get mad. I believe you, you've never seen porno...graphy." Amir and his friends had gotten the best answers they could have asked for, and now it was time to move on to the next question. "The next thing I'm wondering about is pork. I know Islam forbids us to eat pork. But listen to this, Ahmed, I've already told you that Ahmed is crazy. So Ahmed told me at school that pork is just as bad as not eating halal meat. I've seen Muslim friends and other adults eat at McDonald's, Burger King, and other places where the meat isn't halal. If God is in control of everything, why doesn't he just get rid of pork? Why is there pork everywhere?"

"God has said we should not eat pork or animals that are not slaughtered in His name."

"I know that, but you see, our school cafeteria has mostly food with pork, and they don't have halal meat. It's tough being a good Muslim at school. You don't know how it feels when you're hungry, and the only thing you can buy is a cheese pastry with cheese and ham."

"AMIR!"

"Since we're talking about pork, I can also ask about alcohol. Again with Ahmed, you've now understood that Ahmed..."

The other boys could see where this was going and chanted, "IS CRAZY!" Amir looked at his friends and smiled, "Yes, that's right, he's crazy. We have a disco once a month, and you know Ahmed in tenth grade, he's started drinking. I know alcohol is haram and a sin, and that's why we shouldn't drink alcohol. But Ahmed does it with the Norwegian boys, and... why does alcohol exist if it's forbidden?"

The imam was growing impatient and answered briefly, "God has placed all these things on earth to test us."

"Test us? Um... You know what? I can say that Ahmed and many other adults I know have failed that test, big time! But God doesn't say anything about disco, right? I mean, you should see me at the disco; I'm the Pakistani Michael Jackson! The problem is, after dancing as much as I have, and they only serve pizza with pork at the kiosk, it's tough not to eat that pizza."

"Amir..."

"No, really, I'm just saying. It's something God should think about. Maybe God can get the old ladies to serve halal pizza at the disco?" The imam was visibly annoyed; instead of saying his name, he just glared at Amir. "Ok, this is important. When I get older, what if I fall in love with a girl who's not Muslim, what should I do then? Because my dad keeps telling me that I need to find a good Muslim girl and that I should marry in Pakistan... Ok... I'm just going to say it. I like a Norwegian girl in my class, and we think maybe when we get older, we'll get married. I've done thorough research and found out that the Quran says: 'We should treat everyone equally regardless of religion,' 'a Muslim can marry a Christian woman if her faith is pure, she will also have a place with God.' As you can see, I don't care if she's Muslim or not. But am I thinking correctly, God won't be mad at me?"

"If you want to marry a non-Muslim girl, you can convert her to Islam. It's a noble thing to do, and God will reward you for it."

"But what if she doesn't want to be Muslim, or Christian, or belong to any religion at all?"

"Then I recommend you not accept her until she accepts God."

Amir paused and looked hesitantly at the imam. "Isn't it strange that you shouldn't marry the person you love because they don't want to share the same faith as you? Or don't believe at all?"

"A Muslim man should marry a Muslim woman; that's just how it is."

"Okay... It doesn't make sense, but fine. But what if it's a boy who wants to marry a boy? The way I've been taught here at Quran school is that homosexuality is a choice one makes, a sin one commits. But my friend, Kristian in my class, is gay, and he says he didn't choose it himself and can't control who he likes. I get so confused; Kristian is so kind and could have been a good Muslim, doesn't God love everyone?"

Imam - "It's our duty to spread the word of God. Homosexuality is strictly forbidden in Islam, Christianity, and Judaism. A marriage is intended for one man and one woman."

"But if Kristian's body and mind prefer a boy, isn't it God who determines who he should like? Hasn't God decided that Kristian should be gay?"

"AMIR!"

"Right, sorry," Amir muttered, trying to play it cool. "I get it. Our job is to spread the word of God. But what about Jesus? We've started having Religion classes in school, a class where we learn and discuss religion. We've talked a lot about it, but when I went home and asked my father about Jesus, he got really angry. I also asked some other muslims adults at a local Pakistani festival. They got really angry too...So what's the deal with Jesus? Isn't he important in Islam? I feel like we don't pray to God, but to Muhammed. But what about Jes--"

"AMIR!" the imam yelled, cutting him off and saying something in Arabic.

Amir was confused, but the imam switched back to Norwegian to make his point clear. "You shouldn't say the name of our prophet like that, peace be upon him. You should always say Muhammed, peace be upon him."

"Right, my bad," Amir said, sheepishly. "But why do the adults get so angry when I talk about Jesus? Why is Muhammed, peace be upon him, so much more important? I mean, Jesus is mentioned countless times in the Quran...He was a prophet who brought God's message, and that's pretty important, right? Why don't we ever say 'Jesus, peace be upon him?' Doesn't Jesus deserve some peace too? Why is it that Muhammed, peace be upon him, is valued more highly than Jesus?"

The imam's expression softened a bit, as he realized that Amir was genuinely trying to understand. He cleared his throat and began to explain the nuances of Islamic beliefs about prophets and their roles. Amir listened intently, eager to understand more about the religion he had grown up with.

"Our prophet, peace be upon him, was sent by God to restore Islam. Our prophet, peace be upon him, is the reason why we have Islam, and that's why we're so lucky because of him. That's why many Muslims consider our prophet, peace be upon him, holier than Jesus. But Jesus is also important in the Quran. Jesus will come back to earth, fight an important war, and unite all religions under one religion, Islam."

"Come back? So God knows what's going to happen in the future?" Amir asked.

"God knows everything and more than we can imagine," the imam replied.

Amir carefully considered the imam's explanation, sensing that something didn't quite add up. "If God knows everything that's going to happen, that there will be an anti-Jesus, or that there will be wars in his name, then he has already determined from the beginning what will happen to us, right?"

"That's correct. God knows everything," the imam affirmed.

"But then he must have known that his religion would lead to eternal wars around the world, division between Sunni and Shia Muslims, oppression of women, and the misuse of religion to control politics? Or has he planned all of this? If he has, then... I don't know, maybe he's not the God we all think he is?" Amir argued.

Amir noticed that the imam was starting to get angry, but he felt he had a valid point, so he continued. "Ok... Since we're talking about God who knows everything, I'm curious about how paradise actually works. I've heard that if a Muslim dies for God, he will get 72 virgins in paradise. Isn't that a bit strange? If a man gets 72 virgins, does that mean he gets 72 women who will serve him forever? Will they spend their eternal lives satisfying only one man? What if the man who dies is incredibly ugly? Then those poor women will have to sleep with him without having a choice. Or, what if it's a perverted man? Because I'm thinking if Ahmed, who's crazy in the head, dies and gets 72 virgins, those girls are going to be fucked. Ahmed talks about a lot of weird sex positions that none of us in the eighth grade understand."

"AMIR!" the imam shouted.

"Okay, okay... But if men get 72 virgins, do women get the same treatment? I mean, I wouldn't exactly be thrilled to have 72 inexperienced men, it's almost barbaric... Have you ever looked at Pornhub? No, wait, you haven't, but have you heard of bukkake? A bunch of horny men standing in a circle, all jizzing on a poor lady in the middle, everyone with their dicks out, just cum here, cum there, and everywhere..." Amir stood and laughed as he demonstrated bukkake to the boys. This was the final straw for the imam, and he flew towards Amir in a fit of anger.

SLAP

Amir looked up at the imam with a hand over his face. "You shouldn't have done that. You know I'm not a good Muslim to begin with, and hitting me in front of everyone wasn't a good idea." He looked at his shocked and frightened classmates. "What are we doing here? Does no one see how crazy all of this is? Just because I go to a disco and hang out with Norwegian girls, my dad beats me and calls me a bad Muslim.

Is our religion so far up our asses that we can't see how wrong all of this is?"

"AMI...!" the imam yelled.

"Don't 'Amir' me! This is Norway, you can't go around hitting kids here! Should I call child services and tell them you hit me? Oh, you're not so tough now, are you?"

"I don't understand Islam, I just don't. How do you expect us to understand and live by all these rules when not even Muslims can agree on what's true or not? And don't get me started on all the hundreds of other religions that exist in this world, nothing makes sense! I'm so sick of answering questions about Islam that I don't know the answer to. *Why can't you eat pork? Why can't you drink Alcohol? Why does Fatima in 9th grade wear a hijab? Why are women oppressed in Islam? Why are Muslims so strict? Why do Muslims have to pray five times a day?* I DON'T KNOW WHY! That's why I come to you. But you'll get mad like every other Muslim parents and just say, 'that's just how it is.' NO, IT CAN'T JUST BE LIKE THAT! I don't know how to balance being a good Muslim with being a good Norwegian... A good Muslim, a good Christian, a Jew, or an atheist. What about just being a good human being? Can't we treat each other well, regardless of what religion we believe in? I'm so sick of this religious stuff. It's not my job to convert people to Islam, it's not my job to make sure I don't fall in love with a non-Muslim. I don't even know if I believe in God or if I actually want to be a Muslim."

Amir stopped in his tracks and looked around. "Yes, I said it. It's hard to believe in God when everything sounds so damn stupid. Why do we refer to God as HE? Why do we always say he, he, and he? It seems like religion was written by men and only meant for men. I'm just saying, being promised 72 virgins if you die in God's name is madness. What are you supposed to do with 72 women? Have a book club? It's the perfect propaganda to get large groups of men to follow rules and act without questioning. And... that a man can marry multiple women but a woman can only have one man, COME ON. You can't tell me that God said that? When we talk about women in religion, it's always about what they can't do and how they can't dress - women must be exactly like this, or they'll bring shame to the family. If women have to dress according to the religion's standards, doesn't that mean something is wrong with men? Shouldn't men pluck out their eyes for the sake of religion so they can trust their wives instead? It's not like a woman comes and seduces a man, it's a man's dirty mind that thinks these thoughts."

The imam had clearly had enough and raised his hand again.

"What, are you going to hit me again? Do you not think I get enough beatings at home? Your little hand can't hurt me. That's exactly what I'm getting at, you get angry because I ask you questions that you, of all people, should be able to answer. You work for God, who knows everything, so you should have more knowledge than anyone else in the world! But you can't even answer how the universe began, what a black hole or galaxy is, what's on the other side or if there's anything beyond this world. All you can do is refer to those medieval books and just say, 'that's how it is.' We just have to wait for the Day of Judgment, that's what we live for. This is old-fashioned thinking that causes fathers to kill their daughters because they're not good enough Muslims and mothers to be disappointed in their sons when they marry non-Muslim girls. And don't get me started on the Catholics, a bunch of pedophiles. We know that there are imams out there who also screw little kids..." The imam couldn't hold back and slapped Amir once again.

SLAP

Amir laughed at the imam: "The fact that you hit me again says more about your stupid religion. I'm outta here. You can call my dad and complain, I'll gladly take that beating. If God really exists, I'll ask about you and all the other incompetent religious people when I die. Is this really how he wants us to live?" The imam was completely stunned. No one had ever spoken to him like that before.

With the Quran and his shoes under his arm, Amir walked out of the mosque with his head held high. He reached into his jacket pocket and took out a handful of coins - 1 dollar from each of his four sisters and 5 dollars from his dear mother - consolation money for the beating he got from his father the week before. He smiled with joy and realized he had enough money for a movie ticket and a small popcorn.

Amir tried to talk to God one last time after everything that had happened: "For being an idiot, you have at least given me strong female role models. If you really exist, you must have realized it's time to hand over religion to women. If not, it's never going to get better. I don't know if you're an alien, an energy, or just a dumb old man. Either way, you need to get your act together."

Thank You to

First and foremost, I want to thank the talented writer on my team. My good friend Martin Brurås Tønnessen, your language skills and ideas have elevated this book. I cannot thank you enough for the time you have put into these strange stories of mine. The way you have helped me adjust the texts and characters, cut down paragraphs, and pushed me to write new drafts - the result has been impressively good.

I also want to thank my family who helped me through a difficult time. Thank you to my mother and my sisters who have been the backbone of our family, and thank you for not suppressing my voice. Without my older sister Rukshana, I would never have become who I am today. Thank you for always letting me stay with you. Thank you for letting me stay up all night and watch weird movies that I wasn't supposed to watch. Thank you for letting me read sci-fi books that I wasn't supposed to buy. And most importantly, thank you for discussing religion with me without getting angry. You carry your religion with pride, and always let me have my own opinions and values. I can never thank you enough, and I am so happy to have you in my life.

Thank you to my good friend Thomas Kleppe, who read the first draft of the book and gave critical feedback on every text - thank you for always being there. Thank you to Henrik Sommerschild, who drew the illustration for the book cover. (Fun fact; Henrik is the character in the *Day Amir Got Slapped by the Imam*)

Thank you to Lita Hatlestad, Nick Berisha, Angad Singh, Kasim Imtiaz, Petter Anderssen, Omar Noir, Dieu-Donné Elie Nsamba, Nelson K. Miancho, Rawas Moustafa, Ingrid S, and thank you to all of you who listened to my weird stories.

Editor: Martin Brurås Tønnessen
Illustration: Henrik Sommerschild
Translated into English by: Amir Shaheen

ISBN:

Ingram Content Group UK Ltd.
Milton Keynes UK
UKHW040027060523
421309UK00002B/6